MW00490052

THE SIDHE SERIES
THE CIRCLE

BY CINDY CIPRIANO

PRESS

Copyright © Cindy Cipriano 2019

All rights reserved. No part of this publication may be reproduced, stored in or introduced into a retrieval system or transmitted in any form or by any means, electronic, mechanical, photocopying, recording or otherwise without prior written permission from the publisher.

This is a work of fiction. Names, characters, places and incidents are either the product of the author's imagination or are used fictitiously, and any resemblance to any person or persons, living or dead, events or locales is entirely coincidental.

First published by Odyssey Books in 2013

Published by Vulpine Press in the United Kingdom in 2019

Illustrations by Paul Summerfield

ISBN: 978-1-912701-68-1

Cover by Claire Wood

www.vulpine-press.com

For Connor

THE CHANGELING

Deep within the faerie realm
when a babe there cannot be,
I'll snatch you as you sleep my dear
and you will live with me.

My child of laughter, or made to weep
forever you will be.
Your family will forget you,
all alone with me.

Together we will watch the nest,
till death takes the chickadee.
And if those seven years you stay,
you never will be free.

When time has gone, and it's too late,
that's when you will love me.
And with your heart, I'll change your mind
and who you used to be.

For that is how we add our clans,
our servants and family.
The verse once spoken cannot be claimed
and you will be as me.

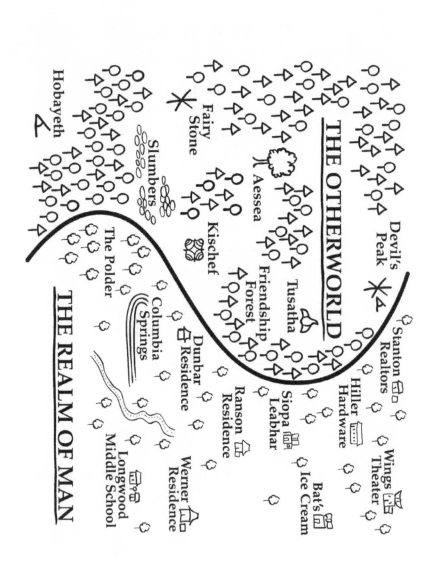

PROLOGUE

As the summer downpour slowed, three boys charged outside to play in the newly created puddles, racing paper boats in ribbons of water that flowed from the house to the road. Covered head-to-toe in mud, the boys loved every minute of it.

Something—a rock? A pebble?—flew out of nowhere, landing in a puddle at Calum's feet. Water splashed into his face and at once he was blinded by an unexpected and intense pain. He rubbed his eyes and called out for help.

"What's wrong?" Hagen asked.

By now, Calum's eyes were on fire. It was hard for him to think of anything else except the searing pain. "Something's in my eyes," he shouted.

"Go rinse it out," said Finley, still slopping away, digging mud from a puddle.

"I can't see anything," said Calum, no longer trying to hide the panic in his voice.

"Come on. I'll help you," said Hagen. He took Calum by the arm, leading him into the house.

Calum's mother, Kenzie, met them in the hallway. To a casual observer, the sight might seem run-of-the-mill, something to be expected when three boys wallow in the mud. Surely it was an ordinary scene that had played out many times in ordinary neighborhoods.

But, Kenzie, Calum, and his cousins are not ordinary people. They aren't actually people at all. Calum and his family are Sidhe, or faeries, and they did not live in an ordinary neighborhood. Calum's home was in Tusatha Mound, one of dozens of faerie mounds scattered throughout the Otherworld.

Like all adult Sidhe, Kenzie was able to read the thoughts of other faeries. She had been monitoring the boys all morning and was alerted by the abrupt change in Calum's emotional state. Kenzie knew something was wrong and she was already on her way outside to check on them when Calum and Hagen staggered into the house.

"Bring him to the kitchen," she said, leading the way.

Kenzie pulled glass vials out of an old wooden case on the floor of the pantry. The tiny bottles were unlabeled, but that didn't slow her down. She settled on three and placed them on the table just as Hagen eased Calum into a chair. Kenzie skimmed the tops of the vials with her fingertips. "This one," she said, snatching the vial up and quickly opening it.

"How do you know?" asked Hagen.

"I can feel its purpose flowing from it," said Kenzie. She stood over Calum, tipped his head back, and carefully applied one drop into each of his eyes.

Calum felt instant relief. The white-hot pain in his eyes was replaced by a cloud-light sensation of cooling comfort. He was perplexed by the speed at which the pain first had come and then gone. Calum blinked once and his vision returned to normal.

"What was it?" asked Hagen.

Kenzie looked into her son's eyes, searching for clues. "I don't know, but it's gone now. Where were you playing when you got hurt?"

"We were over by the—" said Calum.

But Kenzie was out of the kitchen, running toward the front door before Calum finished his sentence. She bolted outside, screaming Finley's name.

CHAPTER ONE

SIOPA LEABHAR

Calum Ranson was sure his cousin Finley was alive and knew he would be the one to find him. After all, it was his fault Finley had disappeared in the first place. Calum rubbed his eyes, as if the gesture would help him remember some clue about Finley's disappearance. Calum often did this while he was deep in thought. It was a nervous habit, a subconscious twitch. And, though his eyes no longer burned, they still held what his mother described as a "phantom" pain.

"Like a memory," she'd said.

A memory, Calum thought. *Just like Finley was becoming. Nothing more than a memory.* He paused briefly, repeating his promise to Finley. *I will find you.*

A gentle tug reminded Calum they were running late. He smiled down at Wrecks, his large black dog. Wrecks' tail was sharply bent at the end, making him look as if he were perpetually taking a right turn. He bounced rather than walked, leading the way down the cracked sidewalks of Emerald Lake. When the pair neared Siopa Leabhar, Wrecks impatiently pulled Calum up the front steps.

Siopa Leabhar was the oldest store and only bookstore in Wander County. No one remembered when it had been built, and that was no accident. Secrets filled the bookstore—secret stories, secret rooms, and secret people.

Calum opened the door and Wrecks bounded in, wagging his tail. He ran to each shelf, or stack, as Calum's mother called them, sniffing everything as if he had never been there before. The stacks were ancient and made of heavy dark wood. Curved seats facing opposite directions were carved into the base of each stack, and the shelves were covered with delicate script.

The words were Italian, providing a record of difficult faerie verses. They were spoken into existence by one of the oldest of faerie clans, the Foletti. Not one surface of the shop was free of the tiny writing.

Finding a particular verse was nearly impossible because the lines constantly shifted. As new lines were added, existing lines spread out like dye in water, moving to accommodate the new faerie verse. Calum first witnessed the never-ending rearrangement of words when he was eight years old.

He was sitting at the checkout desk, wondering if he'd ever master the fine art of bicycle riding. An odd glowing on one of the nearby stacks caught his attention. He moved to get a closer look and found one of the verses pulsing with a soft orange glow. Calum read the verse, quickly realizing it would help him learn to ride his bike. He ran back to the checkout desk for paper and a pencil to copy the lines. But by the time he returned to the verse, the words were drifting to the highest part of the stack. Kenzie had observed Calum's mad dash and took the opportunity to explain that he was not allowed to use his talents to gain any advantage.

When Calum had asked his mother about the glowing, she'd said the verses anticipate the needs of Siopa Leabhar's visitors. "The lines glow when a visitor nears the verse they desire."

And, that's the story they told the tourists.

Emerald Lake was one of many resort towns in the mountains of western North Carolina. In addition to Siopa Leabhar, Specs Optical, and several boutiques, the quaint town was home to Columbia Springs. Tourists invaded Emerald Lake every summer to swim and fish in the cool springs, smugly thinking they knew the best-kept secret of the mountains.

If they only knew, thought Calum.

Along with the ever-moving sea of faerie verse, odd items turned up unexpectedly in Siopa Leabhar. One morning, Calum and Kenzie were surprised to find a large, empty picture frame hanging beside the front door. Faerie verses had shifted and squeezed together to free up the entire space inside the frame, exposing the weathered brick wall. The purpose of the frame was revealed when a customer dropped their keys at the base of the frame, bent to retrieve them, lost their balance, and toppled through the wall.

This prompted one of the few visits by the Foletti. They explained they were testing their idea of putting thresholds, or portals, to the Otherworld in plain sight. "Making the jump between the worlds more convenient for Sidhe who had decided to live in the Realm of Man," the Foletti Sidhe explained.

The Foletti returned the customer, no worse for wear, but minus a bit of her immediate memory. They had decided the convenience of such a threshold was not worth the trouble of accidental visitors. The frame disappeared with the Foletti Sidhe and neither had returned since.

Another time, a key popped up, hanging from an ornate hook on the end of one of the stacks. When Calum grabbed the key, a keyhole materialized, hovering in mid-air. He fit the key into the keyhole and a burst of light shot through, freeing an imp. The imp darted from the bookstore before Kenzie could catch him. Thankfully, the lack of dark Sidhe in Emerald Lake tamed the imp's devious tendencies. He soon learned to adapt to life in Emerald Lake, settling in a mandrake grove on the edge of town. And Calum learned to never touch any "new" item in Siopa Leabhar without first checking with Kenzie.

Calum stepped over the morning mail that had fallen through the slot on the front door. He quickly scooped it up before Wrecks tried to "help."

A slender woman stepped from around one of the tall stacks. Her long brown hair spilled over her shoulder as she bent to plug in the string of white lights framing the shelf.

"Well, good morning, son," said Kenzie Ranson. "Sleepy start?" She turned on antique table lamps as she wove her way between ballooned chairs and puffy ottomans.

"Yeah," said Calum, yawning as he spoke. "Tell me again why I can't take the rest of the summer off and stay home?"

"We've been over this," said Kenzie in a lilting voice. "It's been so busy this season and the tourists seem to be hanging on longer than usual. Besides, you'd get bored sitting around the house all day by yourself."

Calum sighed. He hung Wrecks' leash on a brass hook beside

the door and walked through the cinnamon-scented bookstore toward the shelf where the dog's bed was kept.

"*Accessi*," he said, his hands stretched out before him.

Nothing happened.

He felt his mother's eyes on him as he repeated, "*Accessi*," more forcibly this time. He willed the bed to move from the shelf, but it didn't budge.

Kenzie cleared her throat and busied herself, straightening a stack of magazines.

Calum knew he was slipping. He was losing his Sidhe talents, and he didn't know why. His magic had always been reliable, but over the last few months, something had changed. Calum's talents were unpredictable and weak. Giving up, he dragged the dog's bed down in frustration, dropping it beside the store's only checkout.

The checkout was made of the same dark wood as the stacks, and hundreds of lines of writing covered its surfaces. A dozen crystal vials bounced colorful light across a thin plate of protective glass on the countertop. Kenzie's herbal treatments. A yellowed certificate designating her a Master Herbalist was pinned under the glass plate. The certificate was a fake, but it didn't matter. All of Kenzie's "treatments" worked so well, no one ever questioned her license to practice.

Kenzie walked to the small café at the front of the store. A crescent-shaped light hung from the ceiling, casting a warm glow on the curved counter. Each of the tall and extraordinarily soft chairs would soon be filled as locals drifted in for their morning coffee and baked treats. A half dozen aged diner booths lined the windows of the café, giving it a retro feel. Kenzie clicked on machines that brewed her delicious espressos, coffees, and teas. The house favorite, a sassafras tea, encouraged customers to be loose with their money. Kenzie made sure this tea was available all year long. Iced in the summer, hot in the winter. It was not at all unusual for a customer to come into the bookstore with a craving for sassafras tea, and suddenly remember they needed to buy a book. Or two. A trolley sounded its bell as it rolled by the bookstore on the first of many trips through town.

"Time to open," said Kenzie. She unlocked the door and raised the wooden blinds covering the store's windows.

"But there's nothing to do," groaned Calum. He slumped on the stool behind the cash register, his shoulders drooping low, and picked up a box of price stickers. He removed several and stuck them on the ends of his fingertips. Calum smiled as he remembered the time he and Finley had "decorated" their younger cousin with similar stickers. Even though none of the customers had seemed interested in buying a screaming toddler, both boys were sent to different corners of the bookstore along with several long picture books.

"There's plenty to do," said Kenzie. "You can start by organizing the desk." She pulled a bright orange clearance sticker from his forehead. "The summer reading books are going fast so please unpack the rest of them and add them to the display. Oh, and put these flyers out, too." She handed him a stack of paper.

Calum read one of the lavender sheets.

SHARE YOUR TALENT AT SIOPA LEABHAR.

JOIN US EVERY FRIDAY NIGHT FOR GOOD FOOD AND GREAT MUSIC. COME EARLY AND STAY LATE AS WE SUPPORT OUR

He hung his head at an angle, allowing his light brown hair to fall away from his face. "And then what?"

"And then," said Kenzie, tucking a bit of his hair behind his ears, "you can get a haircut."

"Awesome," Calum said sarcastically. He sighed loudly as he unpacked the books and restocked the shelves, moping about his predicament. As he put the last book on display, the shop bell chimed. Wrecks scurried to greet the customers, his toenails making ticking noises as he slid across the oak floors.

Calum looked up to see a girl with a bouncy blonde ponytail enter the store. She was closely followed by a woman who had the same color hair, the same clear skin, and the same gleaming blue eyes. The woman carried a red-and-white purse, and the girl held a canvas tote bag.

"Good morning," Kenzie said brightly. "Can I help you find something?"

"Yes, please," said the woman. "I registered my daughter at the middle school yesterday. They sent us here to buy her summer reading books."

"Well, welcome to Emerald Lake. I'm Kenzie Ranson."

"Andrea Werner. And this is my daughter, LaurelAnn."

"Laurel," said the girl, rolling her eyes.

"*Laurel* needs to get the summer reading books for rising sixth graders," said Andrea, a hint of exasperation in her voice.

"We've got plenty," said Kenzie, conveying her understanding with a warm smile. "That's my son, Calum." She pointed to him at the checkout desk. "He's going into the sixth grade, too."

Calum was trying to slide off the stool and slink behind the desk. He didn't have much experience talking with girls. Well, not lately. Although he'd known all of the girls in Emerald Lake for most of his life, many of these friendships seemed to change towards the end of the fifth grade. Lots of the girls now seemed silly. They constantly giggled about everything, leaving him clueless in their wake. He supposed this had something to do with all of them heading off to middle school.

"Newcomers get refreshments on the house," Kenzie said in a friendly tone. How about a nice cup of sassafras tea, Andrea?"

Calum smirked at his mother's offer.

Kenzie saw him and added, "Calum can help Laurel find her books."

That was one of the last things Calum wanted to do, save for maybe shutting his hand in a car door. *No matter*, he thought, *she's just another customer.* He led Laurel through the bookstore, pointing out various sections while Wrecks ran circles around her, his tail thumping loudly against the stacks.

"Sorry about him," said Calum.

Laurel shifted her bag. "That's okay." She bent to pet the wriggling dog. "What's his name?"

"Wrecks. With a W."

"W-R-E-C-K-S?"

"Yeah. We named him that because he had really big feet when he was a puppy, and he wrecked everything."

"Cool," said Laurel. "I have a cat, but I've always wanted a dog, too." She continued stroking Wrecks, who seemed to calm at her touch until at last, he sat down on the floor. "Where'd you get

11

him?"

"The animal shelter. He's some kind of mixed-up mutt. Part pit bull terrier and part who knows what." Calum snapped his fingers. "Come on, boy."

"He's sweet," said Laurel, standing to follow them. "So, what's Seo...Sio...opa."

"Shuppa Leb Har," said Calum.

"Yeah, that. What's it mean?"

"It's Gaelic. Siopa means shop and leabhar means book."

"Do you know Gaelic?"

Calum nodded. "Kenzie's from Ireland. She taught me."

"Kenzie?"

"Uh, yeah," said Calum.

It was a Sidhe secret, how they called each other by their first name to strengthen their talents. Calum had spent so much time with his mom at the bookstore, he'd let his guard down, calling her Kenzie in front of Laurel. He tried to think of a cover for his mistake.

"Irish good luck tradition," he stammered.

"Calling your parents by their name?" asked Laurel, puzzled. "I've never heard of that one."

I'm sure you haven't, thought Calum.

"My middle name's Irish, though. Rosaleen. It means beautiful rose." Light pink circles appeared on her cheeks.

"Yeah, I know what Rosaleen means." Calum felt heat rising on his face and he self-consciously scratched the back of his neck.

"Is that what's written all over the shelves? Gaelic?"

"No. That's Italian."

"My cousin told me about that writing. He said—"

"Said what?"

"He said it was magic, or spells…" She trailed off. "And now I feel stupid. He was probably just making fun of me. You know, because we're new here." She shook her head. "So, can you read the words? Do you know Italian?"

"A little." Calum smiled a cockeyed grin. He was intrigued by the Foletti verses, and often wished he were a part of their clan. But one couldn't help the clan they were born into. He glanced at Laurel, who was smiling down at Wrecks. Calum was surprised by how easy it was to talk to her. Maybe she was the non-giggling variety of girl. "So, why did you guys move here? I mean, hardly anyone does."

"My dad's going to be the new assistant principal at Longwood Middle School." Laurel watched him closely as she said this.

The principal's kid.

Calum tired to look cool, but he was never any good at that kind of thing. He felt his face warm again. Thankfully, Laurel looked away.

"What's out there?" she asked, pointing to double glass doors at the back of the shop.

"A garden." Calum believed girls were supposed to like flowers and stuff like that. He wondered if she'd like to see it, but before he could ask, Andrea called her to the café. They joined their mothers who were in the middle of a "getting to know you" conversation over tea and croissants.

"We moved to Emerald Lake to be closer to my husband's

sister, Ellen Spencer," said Andrea. "Do you know her?"

Kenzie nodded. "Ellen's son, John Phillip, has been in all of Calum's classes since kindergarten."

Calum was baffled that Laurel, who seemed perfectly normal, was related to John Phillip Spencer. That kid reminded Calum of a gnat—constantly buzzing around and annoying everyone. He hoped, as he did every year, that John Phillip would not be in any of his classes.

Andrea looked around the bookstore. "You have some nice pieces, Kenzie. This counter is exquisite. And the stacks are obviously handmade. I've never seen a solid piece of wood carved in such a way. The details on everything are amazing. Look at the checkout desk, LaurelAnn. I mean, *Laurel*."

"What's written on it?" asked Laurel. "It looks different than the Italian writing on the shelves."

"It is." Kenzie eyed Laurel suspiciously. "That's Gaelic."

"Here we go," muttered Calum. He knew his mom needed little prodding to launch into telling the story carved on the desk.

"It's a love story called *A Broken Accord*," said Kenzie. "It's about a couple named Aidan and Shona who lived in Emerald Lake. They were young when they fell in love, but it ended badly, maybe because of their age. In the end, Shona died of a broken heart."

Laurel said she wanted to hear more, but Andrea glanced at her watch. "Sorry honey, we need to get a move on and meet your dad." She looked at Kenzie. "He's only here for a few hours before he has to go back to Virginia. We're supposed to meet him at the realtor's office in fifteen minutes."

14

"What about my books?" asked Laurel.

"I'm afraid they'll have to wait," said Andrea.

"If you're talking about Stanton Realtors, they're just a couple of blocks up the street," said Kenzie. "If you'd like, you can leave Laurel here to buy her books, it'll only take a minute. And then Calum can walk her over on his way to the barber shop."

Calum rested his forehead on his palm, hoping his shaggy hair covered his reddening face.

"Please?" begged Laurel.

Andrea considered this as she checked her watch again. "Do you have your cell? Is it on?"

"Yes." Laurel sighed loudly. "I'll be fine."

"All right, but don't you dare take the trolley. I think it goes too fast," said Andrea.

"Okay, *Mom.*"

"I'll send them over in a few minutes," assured Kenzie.

Andrea gathered her purse and left the store, but not without glancing back at Laurel two or three times.

"She's ridiculously overprotective," said Laurel.

"Don't worry about it," said Calum. He hopped off the counter stool and guided Laurel deep into the stacks. "We have to read two books. Do you want both of 'em?"

"Yeah, but first I want to get something else." She looked toward the café where Kenzie was clearing their table. Laurel lowered her voice. "Where are your mythology books?"

"Greek? Roman?" asked Calum.

"More like folklore. Stuff about fairies."

Calum looked at Laurel, trying to measure her sincerity. "Aren't you a little big for fairy tales?"

"Can you please just tell me if you have any books like that or not? If I don't hurry up and get over to that realtor's office, my mom's gonna freak."

"Sorry. Yeah. They're over here." He showed her the Nature and Folklore section.

Given the local legend about the faerie verses carved throughout the store, Laurel wasn't the first customer to ask about fairies. But Calum thought she seemed to have more than a passing curiosity. He tried to smooth things over, hoping she would elaborate. "I guess your mom doesn't like you reading about fairies."

"She doesn't believe they exist, but I know they do."

Calum stared at her hard. She didn't seem to notice. He watched her hand move to her neck. A gray stone with an ill-formed cross hung from a long silver chain. She held onto it as she scanned the titles on the stack, the fingertips of her free hand gliding over the spine of each book.

"I'll try this one," said Laurel. She pulled *An Encyclopedia of Fairies and Other Natural Oddities* from the stack. "I'd better pay for it now." She carried the book to the cash register where Calum scanned the book's barcode.

"That's seventeen dollars and twenty-five cents," he said.

Laurel laid down a handful of money. "I have change." She reached into her pocket and pulled out a quarter. There was a spark and a soft pop as Calum took the coin from her.

"Ouch!" he said, quickly withdrawing his hand.

"It must be static electricity," said Laurel. She tucked the book inside her tote bag along with one of the Talent Night flyers.

"Yeah, I guess," said Calum. *Static electricity? In the summer?*

The shop bell chimed. Andrea Werner was back. "Sorry, kiddo. Your dad wants both of us to look at a house."

"Now?" asked Laurel. "But I didn't get my books yet, and I only have a few weeks to read them before summer's over."

"We'll have to get them later." Andrea looked around the shop for Kenzie. "Would you please thank your mom for me?"

"Yes, ma'am," said Calum. "Do you want me to put the books on hold?"

"No thanks," Andrea said hurriedly. "Laurel and I are staying two doors down at the Whitney Hotel. We'll come back tomorrow."

Calum drummed his fingers on the desk as he watched them leave the store. He wanted to know more about Laurel and her interest in faeries. Or maybe he just wanted to know more about her. Calum wondered what Laurel thought about him, although he didn't know why it should matter. He hid between the stacks, quietly following them through the bookstore, listening to their conversation.

"Well?" asked Andrea, as they approached the door.

"He seems nice," Laurel said in a hushed whisper. "Not at all weird like John Phillip said he'd be. And he didn't seem to mind that Dad's going to be the assistant principal. Maybe I will find some friends here."

"Imagine that," said her mother as they closed the door.

"Imagine that," said Calum. He watched through the window

as a car rolled to a stop in front of the bookstore.

"Imagine what?" asked Kenzie, stepping from behind a nearby stack.

Calum jumped at the sound of her voice, knocking several books to the floor. "Geez, Mom, don't sneak up on me."

"Especially not when you're sneaking up on someone else, right?" A wave of Kenzie's hand caused the books to float dutifully back to their places on the shelf. "You're right to be curious, though. I'm sure you saw it hanging around her neck. I wonder how that girl got a token from one of the darkest of faerie clans. I'd love to get a closer look at it." Kenzie squinted as she watched Laurel climb into the backseat of the Stanton Realtor car.

"I don't think she knows what it is," said Calum.

"Either way, we'd better keep an eye on her."

My summer just got a lot more interesting, thought Calum.

CHAPTER TWO

OLD FRIENDS - NEW FRIENDS

Although he wasn't exactly looking, Calum found an intriguing faerie verse among the hundreds at Siopa Leabhar that morning. He was careful to copy the lines quickly and hoped he'd gotten everything right. But as he wrote down the last few words, the lines began to switch and move. He glanced down at his paper, checking his notes. When he looked back up, he saw the last line of the verse rolling away from him as if it had been written on the crest of a wave.

After they closed the shop for the day, Calum spent the entire afternoon experimenting with the verse, trying to find the right mixture of ground leaves, snakeskin scales, and a light Moroccan spice. He held the end result, a vial of golden dust, in his right hand. The dust was like corn starch, silky and fine, but without the residue. He rooted around a long-forgotten toy box inside an armoire in the living room. Smiling, Calum placed a miniature corvette on the floor and sprinkled some of the dust onto its hood. The tiny red car reared up on its back wheels and raced across the family room.

Buster, Calum's black-and-white cat, took off after the car, but stopped when it sped under the couch. The car crashed into a wall just as the doorbell rang.

This will come in handy, thought Calum. He pocketed the vial, feeling a sense of accomplishment over the success of this new verse. He smiled as he watched his father answer the door. Gus Ranson was tall with an athletic build. He was genuinely kind and told funny, sometimes corny, stories. Calum thought he was the best dad in the world.

"Bryan, glad you guys could come," said Gus.

Bryan Stanton set two coolers on the floor of the foyer and shook Gus' hand. The men were the same height, but Bryan was heavier around the middle. It was getting harder to tell he had once played college football.

"Your yard looks great," said Bryan. "You must have worked on it all spring."

"I worked hard following the shade around the house, that's for sure," said Gus, pointing to a hammock in the front yard.

Bryan chuckled and shook his head.

"Good to see you, Diane." Gus bent to kiss her cheek.

"Hey Arlen, Mr. and Mrs. Stanton," said Calum. He didn't dare call other adults by their first name. Not within earshot, anyway. Arlen nodded a hello. His tanned skin and sun-bleached hair told of many hours playing in the summer sunshine. Calum felt sure Arlen had grown at least a foot since he had last seen him. Okay maybe not a foot, but he had gotten a lot taller.

"Hello, Calum," said Diane. "Are you having a good summer?" She smiled in a syrupy way that made Calum think her face might look friendly, if it were on anyone else.

"Yes, ma'am," said Calum.

"Kenzie's outside," said Gus. He closed the front door and picked up the coolers. Bryan and Diane followed him through the kitchen to the back deck.

"Come on," said Calum. "I just got Hero's Revenge. Let's play." He led Arlen to the game room. "What's Elaine doing tonight?"

"Elaine the Pain decided to spend the night with a friend."

As close as he and Arlen were, Calum barely knew Arlen's younger sister, Elaine Stanton. She rarely came to Calum's house because he had no siblings, no companions for her.

"I got my class schedule today," said Calum. "Did you get yours?"

Arlen pulled a white card from his pocket, and the boys exchanged schedules.

"Yes!" said Calum, pumping the air with his fist. "We're in the same homeroom."

"Yeah, but Ms. Itig's supposed to be really strict," said Arlen.

Calum read over the card. "We also have lunch and PE."

"That's cool." Arlen turned his baseball cap backwards, picked up a yellow controller and plugged it into the game system.

"Are you nervous about the first day?" asked Calum, not meaning to blurt out the question.

"No. Are you?" Arlen laughed. "Come on, Cal. People only get stuffed into lockers on TV."

Calum tried to laugh along with Arlen, but it was forced. In elementary school, they used the wooden cubbies that lined the hallways. Calum knew it was illogical, but he wasn't looking forward to using real lockers. He flipped on the game console and pushed a CD into the system. "So, what've you been up to?"

"Just golf camp, but it was awesome. Chuck Williams was there. He taught us how to putt."

Calum had no idea who Chuck Williams was.

"He's in the PGA, Cal."

Calum's blank expression showed he didn't remember what PGA meant.

Speaking slow Arlen said, "The Professional Golfers' Association. Geez." He lounged on the denim blue couch and quickly tapped buttons on the controller.

"Oh," said Calum. "Well, I spent the first week of vacation at my grandparents' house in South Carolina. We went swimming and took their boat out on a lake."

"Hmm," said Arlen in a bored tone. "Golf camp was really fun. It was a little hard at first, but I met a kid who helped me a lot. He's older than we are, and really cool…a great athlete…I've never seen a better player…" On and on Arlen gushed until at last he ran out of things to say.

Calum saw his chance to change the subject. "Hey, since camp's over, maybe you can come to Talent Night at the bookstore."

"Gee, Cal, that sounds like *real* fun." Arlen smirked. "But I doubt it. I'm only home for a few days. I'm going to a baseball camp. Neal, that's the guy I met, he told me all about it. Oh, I forgot. Neal said he's gonna be moving here in a couple of weeks with his dad. His mom and sister are coming after school starts.

Can you believe that?"

Calum couldn't. Two families moving to Emerald Lake in the same month? He was sure that was unheard of.

Arlen seemed to zone out for a second, engrossed in the video game, blasting his way through the double doors of a dilapidated gray building. Although Calum had known him for years, their conversation seemed stiff and disconnected. He was glad to see Arlen, but there was something different about him. Maybe it was the expensive tennis shoes, the brightly colored polo shirt, or the cocky way he talked.

Arlen had definitely changed.

"Boys," called Diane Stanton. "Supper's ready."

Calum and Arlen joined the adults on the octagonal deck off the Ranson kitchen. The air was heavy with the smell of grilled steaks. Wind chimes hanging from the eaves played their tune, and a glass bird feeder enticed several ruby-throated hummingbirds. Wrought iron gliders and café tables were clustered on the deck, and a green canopy covered the entire space.

Calum hoped to avoid more conversation about Neal, but his hopes were dashed. Kenzie made the fatal mistake of asking Arlen about golf camp. The praises of this wonderful new friend bubbled out again like a backed-up drain. When Arlen's parents shared their oh-so-high opinion of the talented Neal, Calum began to worry he had been replaced.

"He's a great player," said Bryan, passing a bowl of potato salad to Kenzie.

"I was worried Arlen wouldn't make friends there," said Diane. She speared a thick steak from a floral platter and passed the rest to Gus. "I was so happy when he called to tell us about Neal. We met him when the boys got back from camp. Such a sweet young man."

Calum thought he might lose it if he had to hear one more thing about Neal. For the first time ever, Calum looked forward to the Stantons leaving. After they all played a round of Horse, he eagerly carried both of their coolers to the car.

Calum and Kenzie used their Sidhe talents to clean their bright yellow kitchen. Moving under their own accord, several dishtowels feverishly dried plates and drinking glasses. A broom zoomed past Calum and his mother, sweeping debris from the hardwood floor. An empty soda bottle soared from the table toward the back door, landing in a green recycling bin just as the front door flew open.

Calum froze.

"Forgot something," said Arlen. He ran into the living room and snatched his baseball cap from the couch. "Later," he said, closing the front door before Calum could react.

"That was close," said Calum.

"It happens," said Kenzie.

He was surprised by her calm reaction. She'd always warned him to be careful when he used his talents so he would not be discovered. Maybe she never expected someone to come through the house unannounced. *Or maybe she's just relieved to see me using my talents correctly.* He smiled when Kenzie gave a flick of her wrist, bolting the front door.

"Hey," she said. "Is everything all right with you and Arlen?"

"Yeah. Sure. I guess," said Calum, agitated.

Kenzie looked at him with eyebrows raised, inviting further explanation.

Calum obliged with a long and heated rant. "No. It's not okay. Arlen's turned into a jerk. I don't know what happened. All he wanted to talk about was Neal. Neal's great at this. Neal's great at that. And now he's going to another camp with Neal. I probably won't even see Arlen again until after school starts." One of the flying plates slammed into a cabinet, falling to the floor in jagged chunks. "Sorry, Mom."

"It's all right. I'll get it." Kenzie waived her right hand and the broom changed direction. It charged at the broken plate, racing the dustpan to the mess. "I know you're upset. But there are many things you can do that Arlen—or Neal—can't."

"Yeah, lots of things. Too bad Arlen will never know about them."

"You'll be able to tell our secret when you have a friend you can trust with it. You'll know when it's right."

"I know, I know." Calum had heard that all his life, every time he had asked permission to tell someone about his magical abilities and his Sidhe clan. That was the nice thing about Hagen and Finley. Calum could be himself around his cousins.

"You met a new friend this summer, too," said Kenzie.

Calum looked at her as if she had three heads. "Laurel? I just met her today. She's not exactly my friend."

"I'm talking about Kira. You swam with her every day when we were in South Carolina."

"Um, Kira's a girl," said Calum pointedly.

"One day you'll realize how funny that is," Kenzie muttered.

"You boys will make a lot of friends as you go through middle school. Sometimes children grow apart as they move along." She patted his shoulder. "Things will be better when Hagen gets home."

Hagen Dunbar and Arlen Stanton were as different as night and day. While Arlen worked hard to be cool, Hagen just was. It was strange, but seeing Arlen today made Calum miss Hagen, and especially Finley, even more.

Calum was still angry with Arlen when he climbed into bed that night. He was glad he had never told Arlen about the Sidhe. *Stupid jerk, probably would have told everyone by now.* As Calum lay awake, his thoughts shifted from Arlen to Hagen. *Hagen will be home soon. Home from Tusatha, the last place we saw Finley. Maybe he'll have some news.* Calum's mind drifted to earlier in the day and his inability to use even a simple faerie verse to move Wrecks' bed to the floor. *I'm sure of no use.*

Kenzie interrupted his thoughts, entering the room with a glass of Murmur Milke, a Sidhe bedtime drink that induced drowsiness. "I heard you tossing and turning. This will help calm your mind." She put the glass on his bedside table. "Everything all right?"

"I was just thinking about stupid Arlen."

"Want to talk?"

"I don't want to talk about him."

Kenzie sat on the edge of his bed. "About what then?"

Calum took a deep breath. "About the Otherworld. When can we go back?"

"I don't know." Kenzie wore a sad expression, one Calum had

seen every time since he'd asked about returning to their world.

"It's been so long since we've been there I hardly remember anything about the mounds anymore. If we could just go back to Tusatha, I know I'd remember what happened to Finley."

"It's just not safe for us there. You know that." Kenzie sounded tired as she rubbed her eyes.

"But Hagen's family goes there all the time."

"Hagen's family is different. And, Tusatha is their mound."

"So why don't we go to our mound? Why don't we go to Aessea?" Kenzie didn't respond. "Mom, something's happening to me. I think I'm losing my talents. I know you know it. But what you don't know is that when I try to use them, sometimes…I feel sick."

A new kind of worry seemed to cross Kenzie's face. "We'll go back. One day. When I think the time is right."

"If that time ever comes," Calum sulked. The sorrowful look in his mother's eyes softened his resolve. *She still blames herself for what happened to Finley.*

"It's late. We both need to get some sleep. Goodnight, son."

Calum watched her leave and felt a tinge of guilt. "Mom?"

Kenzie turned back to him.

"Thanks for the Murmur."

"You're welcome." Kenzie smiled then closed the door behind her as she left the room.

Calum took a few sips of Murmur Milke and returned it to the table. He picked up a nearby book and began to read. Within minutes his mind was calmer. He drifted into a peaceful, Arlen-free sleep. He did not wake when his book fell to the floor.

27

Nothing smells as good as rain. Except when it's mixed with fresh earth. The mud was slick and deliciously black. Calum felt it seeping through his cracked red boots, working its way between his toes.

Calum and his cousins dug canals from a large puddle at the highest point of the sloping lawn. The long trenches quickly filled with rainwater. The boys would use the canals to race paper boats to the bottom of the hill.

"Hurry up, Finley," said Hagen. "We're almost done over here."

"Hang on, don't start without me," said Finley.

"Ouch!" said Calum. "I've got something in my eye." He rubbed his face with mud-caked hands.

"Cut it out, you're gonna make it worse. Go wash up," said Finley, gouging handfuls of mud from the earth, slopping them beside his canal.

"I can't. I can't see anything. It stings real bad," said Calum, blinking furiously. Tears leaked from his eyes, leaving tracks on his muddy face.

"Come on, I'll help you," said Hagen. "Wait for us to get back, Finley."

Calum was pulled to his feet and dragged down the hill. *Not this time. Not this time. This time we're taking Finley with us.* His eyes burned like fire as he struggled to get out of Hagen's grip. "No. Let me go, Hagen. We can't leave him!"

Calum shot straight up in his bed, his heart hammering

against his chest. He heard his cat purr and felt its paws kneading his leg. "Just a dream," Calum muttered. "Just a dream." He wiped salty tears from his face and gulped the rest of the Murmur Milke, falling back to sleep as soon as his head hit the pillow.

The next morning, Laurel and Andrea were added to the list of regulars who enjoyed their morning brew at Siopa Leabhar. Like many others, Andrea had fallen in love with Kenzie's sassafras tea; Laurel the hot chocolate. They usually arrived at the end of the morning rush and stayed for an hour or so. After a week of this, Andrea took Kenzie up on her offer to leave Laurel at the bookstore while she continued house hunting.

Calum was pleasantly surprised when he found himself looking forward to Laurel's visits. When they took Wrecks for walks, Calum made sure their brief bits of freedom conveniently ended at Bat's Homemade Ice cream Shop. The owners of the shop, Frank and Helen, called themselves Calum's adopted grandparents. They always kept his favorite flavor, chocolate curl, on hand and it soon became Laurel's favorite as well.

"You and Laurel seem to be hitting it off," said Kenzie on Friday afternoon as they closed the bookstore for the night.

"She's all right," said Calum.

"Wait. Could it be that a girl could also somehow be a friend?" Kenzie grinned.

"I guess."

"That's good to hear, with her family moving into the neighborhood and all. Something tells me we'll be seeing a lot of Laurel." Kenzie's next words were cautious. "So listen, her parents are going back to Virginia next week to get the last of their things, but she thinks it will be easier on Laurel if she stays here."

"Is she gonna stay with John Phillip?" Calum wondered if she'd still be able to come to the bookstore.

"No, the Spencers will be on vacation."

"Oh, Mom, you didn't." Calum already knew the answer. He groaned. "It'll be weird having a girl stay at our house."

"Don't be silly. Besides, I think she likes you. She told me she likes your haircut." Kenzie playfully nudged him.

"Terrific," Calum said gloomily.

"Andrea doesn't know anyone else in town. And she feels comfortable with us because they've been spending so much time at the bookstore."

"Andrea feels comfortable with us because you make her feel comfortable. I've watched you put calming dust in her tea."

"Guilty," said Kenzie. "She is wrapped pretty tightly. But I do like her. And there's something about Laurel."

"So it's already been decided. Thanks for asking me."

But Calum didn't mind, really. He'd known there was something special about Laurel since the day she reached for the faerie book. Like it held the answer to some riddle. He'd known because he'd recognized the look of someone searching desperately for something lost.

CHAPTER THREE

NO STORM

Laurel and her mother arrived at Siopa Leabhar the following Monday, just before closing. Laurel had red-rimmed eyes and carried a suitcase in one hand. Her other hand held a long leash, which was attached to a black-and-white cat. Calum avoided Laurel's gaze, embarrassed by her display of emotion. He felt suddenly shy and didn't know what to say to her.

Andrea set an empty cat carrier on the floor. "This is for when Whisper needs to ride in the car," she explained. Andrea's eyes always matched Laurel's even today. She tried to secretly wipe a tear from her check as she clumsily handed Kenzie a pink piece of paper. "Here's a list of phone numbers where you can reach us."

"She'll be fine." Kenzie placed a cup of herbal tea in Andrea's hand and wrapped an arm around her shoulders.

"You're right, of course," said Andrea, sipping the tea. "Thanks again for letting her stay with you."

"It's really no trouble. You'll be back before you know it. And we'll keep Laurel busy until then. Here, let me have Whisper. There's lots for him to explore." Kenzie took the leash from Laurel and led the cat away. "Calum, get Laurel's suitcase so they can say their goodbyes."

Calum carried the suitcase to the desk, glancing back in time to see Andrea hug Laurel close. Laurel clung to her mother for several long seconds before looking into her eyes. Andrea stroked Laurel's cheek and lifted the chain that hung around Laurel's neck. She kissed the pendant, and then kissed Laurel on the forehead.

"Remember, we're picking you up on Friday." Andrea hugged Laurel again before she left the store.

That must be what it's like for Finley's mom, Dara, thought Calum, pretending to straighten the books on a nearby shelf. *Except Andrea will see Laurel in a few days, but Dara doesn't know if she'll ever see Finley.*

"Dara will see Finley again," whispered Kenzie. "We all will."

Calum hated that his mother could read his mind. Hated that all adult Sidhe could read his mind. It was one of the talents Calum had yet to develop and at the rate he was going, he doubted he ever would.

"Laurel looks like she could use a distraction. A walk might do her some good. Why don't you guys take Wrecks out while I close up? Go get some ice cream." Kenzie removed Whisper's leash and the cat took off like a shot.

Calum and Laurel made their way to Bat's Ice Cream Shop. In his head, Calum carried on the beginnings of several conversations, but he couldn't find the right words to break the silence.

After several agonizing minutes, Laurel finally spoke. "Sorry for the drama back there."

"Don't worry about it," said Calum. "I was afraid the first time I stayed in a different state without my parents, and I was staying at my grandparents' house."

"I'm not afraid to stay here without them," sniffed Laurel.

"Oh. Well, that's good to know." Calum smiled weakly. *Maybe I should change the subject.* "Um, Kenzie says your parents will be back in time for Talent Night. My dad's bluegrass band's gonna play." Calum paused for a reaction from her. When she didn't respond, he continued. "Hagen'll be back by then. He's in Ireland visiting his grandparents. He's not like you and me. I mean, he's not an only child. Hagen has a brother and a sister."

Laurel began to cry.

I'm really bad at this being friends with a girl thing. "Hey, we can go back to the bookstore if you want," Calum offered awkwardly. *Maybe mom would know what to do with a crying girl.*

"No." Laurel wiped her face. "I'm okay, really. It's just, I'm not like you. I mean, I had a brother. Have a brother. Daniel. We're twins. That's why I didn't want to go back to Virginia. I just couldn't be there while they moved all of our stuff out. I never wanted to leave the place where my brother lived with us. I'm afraid he'll come looking for us and we won't be there."

Calum waited for her to continue, but this time the silence was broken only by the sound of Wrecks' feet skipping over the sidewalk. When they arrived at Bat's, Frank greeted them warmly.

"Hey, Calum, Laurel. Hey, Wrecks, you better check yourself before you wreck yourself." Frank laughed, tossing a dog biscuit to the bouncing dog. Calum and Laurel ordered double scoops of chocolate curl and sat at a cozy booth. Wrecks sat beside Frank, eagerly getting his fill of dog treats. Sunlight streamed through a nearby window, making the green-colored walls of the shop as bright as the lime sherbet in Frank's display case.

"I'd give anything to have Daniel back," said Laurel. She set her empty dish on the glass table and looked into Calum's eyes. "He was here one second and gone the next. Most of the time, I still can't believe it even happened at all. Other times…" Laurel turned to stare out the window. She drew a deep breath and continued, "Other times, I just wish it were me instead. You have no idea how that feels."

"Yeah, I kinda do. My cousin, Finley…" Calum felt a small punch in his belly when he said Finley's name, "He disappeared."

"What? What happened to him?"

Calum had never talked to anyone outside of his family about Finley. But that's not why he didn't tell her. Calum didn't think about Finley as much when Laurel was around. And as bad as Calum felt about that, he needed a break from his guilt over Finley's disappearance. "Some other time."

"Tell me about Hagen then."

"Hagen moved here from Ireland when he was five. He lives in our neighborhood, too. My mom and his dad are cousins. They grew up together in Ireland."

"What about your other friend?"

"Arlen?" Calum hadn't seen or heard from Arlen since the night the Stantons came for supper, and it sounded funny saying his name out loud.

"Yeah. Is he coming to Talent Night?" asked Laurel.

"I doubt it. He's probably at another sports camp. Besides, Hagen and Arlen don't hang out together."

"Why not?"

"They can't stand each other." For the first time this struck Calum as funny. He laughed and shook his head.

"Those are some friends you have." Laurel smiled. She pushed a bit of her hair behind her ear. The strands reflected the sunlight, shining like liquid gold.

Calum smiled back at her. He decided he liked her better when she wasn't crying.

They finished their ice cream and took their time walking back to Siopa Leabhar. When they returned, they found Kenzie finishing a hand-lettered sign.

SIOPA LEABHAR WILL BE CLOSED ON SATURDAY

FOR A FAMILY CELEBRATION.

PLEASE COME BACK AGAIN.

"What's that about?" asked Calum.

"Since your cousins are coming home Friday, we're going to take Saturday off and spend some time with them," said Kenzie. Turning to Laurel, she added, "You'll meet them at Talent Night."

Now it was Laurel's turn to be shy. She fingered the stone pendant on her necklace.

"Don't worry," said Calum. "They'll like you."

"That's an interesting charm on your necklace." Kenzie leaned toward Laurel for a closer look. "Do those marks mean anything?"

"I don't know. Someone gave it to me a long time ago," said Laurel.

"The cord looks frayed," said Kenzie. She cut the air almost imperceptibly with the index-finger of her right hand, and Laurel's pendant crashed to the floor as if being pulled by a strong magnet.

35

Instinctively, Calum bent to retrieve the necklace, but it wouldn't budge. The token seemed to be fused to the ground.

"This is going to sound strange," said Laurel, "but I'm the only one who can pick it up." She retrieved the necklace, placed it back around her neck, and tied the cord. "Mom says it's like the necklace knows I'm its owner."

"Well, it sounds special, that's for sure," said Kenzie, ignoring Calum's questioning glance.

"We better get Whisper in his crate," said Calum.

"Whisper," said Laurel. "I forgot he was here. Is he all right?"

"He's fine," said Kenzie. "He's upstairs in the loft. He's been watching the door, I guess waiting for you guys to come back. Just take the stairs behind the café, you'll see him."

Laurel trotted up to the loft to retrieve her cat. Moments later, she returned cradling Whisper in her arms. "He's not happy with me. I'm sorry, Whisper," she cooed.

Calum drew a sharp breath when he saw the cat up close, "That's weird."

"What?" asked Laurel.

"His markings are the exact opposite of my cat," said Calum. "Whisper has a white triangle on his chest. My cat, Buster, has a black one in the same place."

Whisper slowly blinked, as if this was old news.

Calum loaded Laurel's suitcase into the trunk of the car while Laurel put Whisper's crate in the middle of the backseat. Calum smiled as he watched her strap the crate in with the seatbelt.

Laurel blushed. "We keep each other safe," she said.

"I get it," said Calum. He'd thought any cat who didn't mind wearing a leash wouldn't mind the short car ride to his house on Stone's Throw Road. He was wrong. Whisper howled the entire way, his guttural cries interrupted by an occasional hiss if Kenzie turned a corner too sharply.

"That's it," said Calum, relieved the ride was nearly over. He pointed to the end of the street to a tall storybook house surrounded by yellow bush daises.

Kenzie pulled into the garage and parked. "Show Laurel where to put her things then introduce Buster and Whisper. Hopefully, they'll get along."

Calum led Laurel inside and up a winding staircase. "Your room's up here. It's the one Hagen's sister uses when they stay over."

The room was quite large. Two full-sized sleigh beds covered with matching pink bedspreads made an L in one corner. A dressing table with a pale pink skirt stood in the opposite corner.

Calum thought the room was way too girly. "I hope it's okay."

"Are you kidding?" asked Laurel. "It's so pretty."

"The bathroom's over there," Calum pointed to a door beside the window. He set her suitcase down, and Laurel opened Whisper's carrier. The cat darted from the room and down the stairs in a black-and-white blur.

"Come on," said Calum. "I'll show you where everything else is." He led her to the third floor. "This is my room."

An oversized sleigh bed sat in the middle of the room. An open laptop on the desk flashed a screen saver of three young boys, arms draped around each other's shoulders, huge grins on their faces. Calum, Hagen, and Finley. Calum smiled, remembering the day the picture was taken, but then he noticed a pair of underwear sticking out one of the drawers in his armoire. He roughly closed his bedroom door, hoping Laurel hadn't seen them.

"My parent's room is over there." He nodded to a closed door at the end of the hall.

Kenzie called from the base of the stairs. "Calum, would you please get some oregano for the spaghetti sauce?"

"It's in the sunroom," said Calum. "I'll show you."

The sunroom smelled of damp soil and was full of vegetables, fruit plants, and delicate herbs. Windows stretched from floor to ceiling, bathing the room in warm sunshine. Calum grabbed a pair of small scissors and cut leaves off one of the many tender plants.

"That's strange," said Laurel. "My mom said grown cats don't usually make friends right away. She said our cats might even fight, but look at those two."

Calum glanced at the loveseat where Buster and Whisper sat side by side, sharing a patch of sunlight. A low rumbling distracted him. "That's the garage door. My dad's home."

He led Laurel to the kitchen where, to his horror, he found his parents kissing. Calum blushed deeply as he put the oregano leaves into a small white dish.

"Now, my mind's running crooked today," said Gus, turning away from Kenzie. Although he was Southern, Gus didn't normally have a trace of an accent. He did, however, reserve a special Southern drawl for times that provided maximum embarrassment for Calum. This was one of those times.

"Who's this young lady? She ain't your wife, is she?" he asked in a fake country-boy accent.

Calum responded by turning three darker shades of red.

"Nah, that can't be right," said his country dad, scratching his head. "I don't remember goin' to your weddin'. Maybe she's that move star—Starry McStar."

"Funny, Dad," said Calum. "You know it's Laurel."

"Of course," said Gus in his normal voice. He shook Laurel's hand. "You make yourself right at home. But you'll have to excuse me. I have to get the yard mowed before supper, or the boss won't feed me." He winked at Laurel before leaving the kitchen.

"Your dad's funny," whispered Laurel.

"Yeah. Super hysterical," said Calum.

An hour later, they all enjoyed their meal outside on the deck. Wrecks lay under the table, noisily chewing a stick to pieces. "Cut it out, Wrecks," said Calum. "We'll play fetch after supper."

"Mrs. Ranson…" said Laurel.

"Call me Kenzie."

"Okay." Laurel smiled at her. "Kenzie, I saw some wooden sticks in a vase in the game room. Are those for Wrecks?"

Calum gave his mom a quick glance. He had forgotten to put them away before Laurel arrived.

"Nope, they're not for Wrecks. They're for us. Those are Particulars and they're actually quite rare. That set has been in our family for almost a hundred years," said Kenzie.

"What are they used for?" asked Laurel.

"They predict the future," said Kenzie matter-of-factly.

Gus coughed and looked at her in disbelief.

"Cool," said Laurel. "How do they work?"

"Go get 'em and I'll show you," said Kenzie.

"Are you sure that's a good idea?" Gus asked as soon as Laurel was out of earshot.

"It's fine," said Kenzie. "She'll think it's just a game. Besides, I'm curious about her."

Laurel returned and set a green vase on the table. It was filled with wooden twigs in varying lengths and colors. Some straight, others twisted.

"Draw the one that calls to you," said Kenzie.

Laurel examined the twigs and chose a honey-colored one that was thinner than the rest.

"This makes sense," said Kenzie. "Secrets. You're going to tell one and learn one."

"So cool," said Laurel. "Are the predictions always the same? I mean for the same person, or if I do it again will I get a different prediction?"

"No," said Kenzie. "It depends on a lot of things: the date, the moon's phase, who's drawing the twig, and what's in their heart."

"You do it, Calum," said Laurel.

Calum shrugged. He'd done this hundreds of times, but it had been awhile. Calum studied the twigs and drew a yellow one decorated with golden circles. He handed it to Kenzie.

Her eyes met Calum's as she said, "Rescue."

Calum stared at the twig.

Finley?

On Wednesday, business was slow due to a messy, drizzling rain. Calum sighed as he and Laurel finished their third game of chess. Although he enjoyed getting to know Laurel, having her beside him all day had severely limited his ability to use his talents. Everything seemed to take so much longer; cleaning up the store before going home, washing dishes, and other chores all cut into Calum's free time. He hadn't really thought about how often he used his talents, and even though they were sometimes unpredictable, he found life was dull without them.

He glanced at Kenzie hopelessly. *Nothing to do.*

"I've got something for you guys." Kenzie rummaged through a drawer in the checkout desk. "I bought these for a day like today. Two tickets to Wings Theater to see *Stencils*."

Calum was impressed by his mother's talents. He knew the tickets weren't there when he made change for Mrs. Pennysmith. For once, Kenzie's mind-reading ability proved helpful.

Kenzie gave him the tickets, and pulled two ten dollar bills from the cash register. "For snacks," she said, handing one to Calum and Laurel.

"Awesome," said Calum. "I heard that's a cool movie."

"Thanks, Mrs…I mean, Kenzie." Laurel reached out her arms to hug her, but hesitated.

Kenzie pulled her into a gentle embrace. "You're welcome. If you leave right now, you might just make the next showing."

Calum and Laurel rushed out of Siopa Leabhar, ran down the sidewalk, and right into a long line of people waiting to buy tickets. "It's not a good day for sightseeing. So many tourists," said Calum, looking at the unfamiliar faces.

"But we can go straight in," Laurel said brightly. "We already have our tickets."

As she pulled Calum by the hand, it occurred to him that he had never been to the movies with a girl before. Well, he'd been with Hagen's little sister, but that wasn't the same. Laurel released Calum's hand as they stood before the concession stand menu.

"Everything's so expensive," said Laurel.

"We could split a popcorn," Calum suggested automatically. He and his cousins often did this at the theater. Calum's face flushed. *She's gonna think that's weird.*

"Yeah, let's. And let's split one of those big sodas, too. We can use the rest of our money on candy." Laurel grinned at him.

Calum and Laurel filled up on popcorn, licorice, and chocolates as they watched the movie. Calum wished he'd brought a light jacket. It always got so cold in the theater. But he warmed up when Laurel lifted the dividing armrest to sit closer to him during the scary parts of the film. When the movie was over, the tourists left in cars with license plates from nearby states, and Calum and Laurel walked back to Siopa Leabhar.

"That was pretty good," said Calum.

"Yeah, but all that stuff about copying people is kinda creepy," said Laurel.

They walked a few minutes in silence when a foul odor filled Calum's nostrils. He looked around and then up at the clouds. "Something's wrong. The air smells funny, and it's so sticky." He pulled his T-shirt away from his chest where sweat had caused it to cling to him. "There's gonna come a storm."

As they continued walking, they unconsciously moved closer together. Calum realized they were alone on the street. Not one bird chirped, or even one fly buzzed near them. He jumped when he felt Laurel take his hand. Calum saw the awning at Siopa Leabhar, but it seemed miles away. It was too quiet.

"Calum," called a gruff voice. Frank appeared in the doorway of Bat's. "You two get in here. Now!"

The silence broke with an ear-splitting roar. Calum felt Frank's strong hands as Laurel's scream matched the roaring noise. Frank shoved him inside Bat's, herding them downstairs to the cellar where several other people were already huddled. Frank nearly landed on them when he came thundering down the steps. Calum and Laurel squeezed into the room. Out of the corner of his eye, Calum saw Frank move quickly to Helen's side and put his arm around her. Someone prayed softly in the musty room. The only light went out, plunging them all into total blackness. The windows rattled until Calum thought they would burst, but it was over in ninety seconds. It was over before Calum had a chance to catch his breath or understand what had even happened. The light flicked back on.

"Are you two all right?" asked Frank. Calum and Laurel nodded. "A tornado. I can't believe it. I don't think we've ever had one."

"Not as long as I can remember," said Helen.

"How did you know we were out there?" asked Laurel.

"I didn't. I just had a feeling someone needed help," said Frank.

Kenzie.

"I've got to go check on my mom." Calum bolted up the stairs and out the door, Frank huffing loudly behind him, trying to catch up. Once outside, Calum stopped dead in his tracks. He looked up and down the street. Aside from a few overturned potted plants in front of Hiller Hardware, nothing looked out of place. Laurel and Frank joined him on the sidewalk.

"Are you sure it was a tornado?" asked Calum.

"I grew up in Illinois," said Frank. "We used to have 'em all the time. The sky turned green and it got muggy. Everything was right for a tornado, except..."

"Except what?" asked Laurel.

"Hail. Now that I think about it, there wasn't any hail."

Kenzie walked toward them, looking curiously calm for someone who had just experienced a tornado. Calum noticed the potted plants righted themselves, spilled soil streaming back into the pots, as his mother approached.

Kenzie looked directly into Frank's eyes. "That was some freak storm, wasn't it?"

"I'll say," said Frank, with a dazed look. "Some freak storm."

"He got us into the cellar just in time," said Laurel.

"Thank you, Frank," said Kenzie, still holding the man's gaze.

"No problem. Although it looks like it wasn't necessary. Strange, blustery weather," Frank said, shaking his head as he returned to his ice-cream shop.

That was no storm, thought Calum. *Why did you make Frank think it was?*

Kenzie looked at him and shook her head. "I'm glad you guys are okay. Your mom would probably kill me if I returned you in less than perfect shape, Laurel. Which will be sooner than you thought." Kenzie smiled. "Your dad called. They got back from Virginia right after you two left for the movie."

"All right! I mean, it was fun staying with you guys, but…"

"Don't be silly. I know what you mean," said Kenzie.

"Is that our truck?" asked Calum. He pointed to a gray king cab parked in front of Siopa Leabhar.

"I asked your dad to bring Laurel's things and Whisper," said Kenzie. "Business is so slow today. I thought we'd close up early and take Laurel home."

Something's wrong, thought Calum. Kenzie never closed early. She believed regular hours were the key to regular customers. His mind raced with suspicion. *What's going on?* He looked at her for an explanation.

Kenzie mouthed the words, "Not now."

Calum felt her following closely behind him as they walked down the sidewalk.

At the bookstore, Gus was leaning on his truck, holding Wreck's leash. The dog strained to get to Calum. "Unusual weather we're having," said Gus, handing the leash to his son.

Calum looked up at the clear blue sky as he and Laurel climbed into the cab. Wrecks clumsily jumped in, first trying to sit on Calum's lap, and then settling between Calum and Laurel. Whisper was in his crate, strapped in the front seat. He started his symphony of angry cat expressions as soon as Gus cranked the engine.

45

When they arrived at Laurel's house, Gus had barely stopped in the driveway before Laurel jumped out. She hurried up the brick walkway and through the front door calling, "Mom, Dad, I'm home."

Calum and his parents followed her, carrying her belongings. Calum set Whisper's crate down just inside the door. The home had a warm feel, and a spicy vanilla scent played at Calum's nose. Stacks of unpacked boxes blocked the foyer.

"I'm Rob," said Laurel's dad, maneuvering through clutter. He was quite tall and had reddish brown hair. His eyes were a lighter blue than Laurel's, but they held a deep sadness. He shook Gus' hand. "Thanks for making Andrea and Laurel feel so welcome here."

"No problem," said Gus.

"Everything settled?" asked Kenzie.

"We're getting there," said Andrea. "Come on in. We're taking a break."

"I wish we could, but we've got to get going," said Kenzie. "Calum's cousins are coming home from Ireland. They should be here anytime."

Hagen's coming come today? Calum tried not to look surprised by this news.

"Can we have a rain check?" asked Gus.

"Of course," said Andrea.

"Guess we'll see you at Talent Night then." Gus ushered Calum toward the door.

"Looking forward to it," said Rob.

Calum gave Laurel a half-hearted wave as they walked outside.

The Ranson family climbed back into their truck and drove home.

"Why is Hagen coming back early?" asked Calum.

"I called them," said Kenzie.

Calum knew what that meant. His mother hadn't called them by means of a telephone. There were no phones in the Otherworld with their clan, the Tusatha. Kenzie had used *the calling*, a secret form of Sidhe communication.

"But why did you call them? What's going on?" asked Calum.

"I called them because you were right," said Kenzie. "That was no storm."

Chapter Four

The Reunion

Calum heard the Tusatha calling as he and his parents sat at the kitchen table, awaiting the arrival of the Dunbar family. "They'll be here in a few seconds," he said.

Although Gus couldn't hear Sidhe calls, it was impossible for him to ignore his wife's squeals of joy when the first of five people passed through an invisible threshold in their kitchen. Kenzie gave Tullia Dunbar a fierce hug, and the room came alive with the sound of simultaneous and fragmented conversation. "It's about time," "I've missed you," and "Did you bring your schedule?" carried through the kitchen. After exchanging hugs all around, the adults settled themselves at the table.

"*Ceno*," said Kenzie. Cold cuts, various cheeses, thick baguettes, and small cakes filled an empty serving tray on the counter. Calum and Hagen took their time making sandwiches to eat in Calum's room. Brytes and Will, Hagen's little sister and brother, grabbed snacks and took off for the family room. Weeks without television had made them hungry in a different way.

"Tell us how everyone's doing," said Kenzie. "How are Aine and Connor?"

48

"Yes, how is *the queen?*" asked Gus.

"Gotta love the royal family," said Donnelly Dunbar, wrapping his arm around his wife's shoulder. He was tall like Gus, but Donnelly had a dark complexion and an intense nature.

"Mom's fine," said Tullia, tucking her black hair behind her ears. "She was a bit stressed when the Additions Law was up for review, but she's good now."

At this, Calum made a great show of getting sodas from the refrigerator and passing them to Hagen. The adults seem surprised to see the boys were still in the kitchen. Hagen excused himself and Calum followed, but he stopped in the hallway. He peered around the corner and continued to eavesdrop.

"I thought Additions were outlawed after Finley disappeared," said Gus.

"They were actually outlawed an hour before he disappeared," said Tullia. "But Sidhe laws are reinterpreted every seven years. The Summit was yesterday at the Foletti Mound."

"There was some resistance from the usual suspects," Donnelly said, disgusted. "But the law did pass again. So for now, it's still illegal for Sidhe to add human children to their clans."

"Call it what it is," said Kenzie. "Kidnapping. You mean it's still illegal for Sidhe to kidnap human children."

"There was one small change to the law. An addendum," said Tullia. "It's now impossible for any Sidhe to stay inside a sealed mound for one hour."

"Why the change?" asked Kenzie.

"To protect the *merchants*," said Donnelly, using air quotes around the word.

"He's talking about the black market," Tullia explained. "We'll never stop Sidhe who want trade with the dark clans; there's just too much money to be made. But the new law will protect them inside a sealed mound."

"How, exactly?" asked Gus.

"They come back after one hour. Dead or alive," said Donnelly.

"It's easy to trace which clan is responsible. Too many bodies credited to one clan and no one will trade with them," said Tullia.

"So, you see, things are much safer now," said Donnelly.

"Don't start." Kenzie's voice barely concealed a warning.

"Come on, cuz. It's not healthy for Calum to be away from our world for so long," said Donnelly. "And with the new law, it really is much safer."

"I'll think about it," said Kenzie.

"Don't just say you will to shut me up," said Donnelly. "Really think about it. It's going to become painful for Calum if he stays away too much longer. And, he will eventually lose all of his talents. Besides, his grandparents must miss him."

"My parents come here all the time. So Calum's not missing out on his grandparents," snapped Kenzie.

"But Calum's twelve now," said Donnelly. "He can go to the Otherworld anytime he wants. And he's not limited to the Aessea or Tusatha Mounds. It's just a quick walk through this threshold to the polder, and then he's free to go to any number of mounds."

"I hear you, cuz," Kenzie said in an irritated tone.

"Do you? I mean, Calum's a great kid and all, but he's still a kid. One day he'll go back, with or without your blessing," said

Donnelly. "And when that happens, he won't be prepared. It's better if you take him back now. Let him get used to our ways again."

"That's enough," Gus said impatiently. "That's not why Kenzie called you here."

"Tell us then," said Tullia, trying to diffuse the situation.

Calum listened as Kenzie described the storm. Hearing nothing new, he bolted upstairs. "*Accessi*," he said as he entered his room. He was relieved when his school schedule drifted off his desk and floated toward him. It always embarrassed him when his Sidhe talents didn't work properly in front of Hagen.

"Please excuse my boarding house reach," said Hagen, snatching Calum's schedule from the air. He laughed at his joke and handed Calum his own schedule.

Hagen was a little taller than Calum and had a much darker complexion. Hagen and his siblings inherited their skin color from their dad, and the blackest of black hair from their mom. Tullia had gray eyes and Donnelly's were brown, which explained the unique hazel-colored eyes of their children.

"Let's see," said Hagen. He read over the card as he ate his ham and cheese sandwich. "We're on the same team. And our schedules look pretty much the same. The only difference is PE. I have Coach Miller, but you have Coach Payne. Boy, he sounds rough."

"Yeah," Calum laughed. "Hey, Arlen's on our team, too."

"Thrilling," muttered a non-thrilled Hagen. "Don't tell me he developed a love of music and signed up for orchestra."

Calum answered through a mouthful of potato chips. "No, he

51

didn't. And Arlen doesn't have science or language arts with us, but he's in my PE class."

"How lucky for you," said Hagen, reaching for his soda. "Tullia said some girl was staying here. What's her name?"

The question caught Calum off guard, and he felt his throat tighten. He sipped his soda before answering. "Laurel. She was supposed to stay here a couple more days, but her parents got back early."

"Fess up, cuz," said Hagen. "Your mom told my mom Laurel's cute. Is she?"

"She's okay, I guess." Calum felt heat rising on his cheeks.

"What's she think about Arlen?"

"They haven't met. Arlen hasn't been around all summer."

"I better make friends with her fast, before she moves to the dark side."

"Very funny," said Calum. "Arlen's not that bad. You just need to give him some time."

"It's been years, Calum. It ain't gonna happen," said Hagen.

A long silence stretched between them. "You aren't really going to make me ask, are you?"

"No," said Hagen. He sighed loudly. "There's nothing new about Finley. I'm beginning to think we'll never find him."

"Don't say that." Calum said, pointing at Hagen. "Ever." He walked to the window and stared out.

"In case you've forgotten, I was there too. We were only inside a few minutes, Calum. No one saw anything. It's like Finley evaporated."

"Doesn't matter. Just don't ever say that."

"Okay, okay. I'm sorry. All right?"

Calum studied Hagen's face. Didn't he understand how important it was to never give up hope?

"Hey, I've got something to show you," said Hagen, grinning wickedly. "I got this when we were in Tusatha." He pulled a seed from his pocket, placed it on the carpet and said, "*Cresco.*"

A thick tree trunk materialized, crashing through Calum's bedroom floor. He stared in amazement as he shrank back from the branches of a fully grown loblolly pine. Its top brushed Calum's bedroom ceiling, leaving green streaks on the white paint.

"Awesome." Calum stretched out his hand, feeling the tree's prickly needles. "But how do we get it out of here?"

"It'll disappear in a minute," said Hagen.

"Ha-*gen!*" shouted a voice from below.

"Sounds like a minute's not fast enough," said Calum. They raced each other back to the kitchen where the pine's trunk stood in the middle of the room. Gnarled roots pulsed as they worked their way through the floor.

"Look at this mess," Tullia said sternly.

The tree abruptly vanished.

"What mess, Tullia?" Hagen asked innocently.

Gus and Donnelly burst out laughing.

"Don't encourage them," said Tullia. A snort broke through her suppressed laughter, causing everyone else to laugh harder.

"*Cresco.* I'd forgotten that one," Donnelly chuckled. "Anyway, I was about to call you guys down. I want to hear more about this storm."

Calum described the strange weather he'd experienced earlier that day with Laurel, and how Frank was convinced there had been a tornado.

"So, what do you think, Donnelly?" asked Gus.

"I think a tornado with no wind, no hail, and no damage is no tornado. You were right, Kenzie. I can feel it. Dark Sidhe have come to Emerald Lake."

Wi

It was standing room only in Siopa Leabhar on Friday night. The many conversations of tourists and locals made a low buzz in Calum's ears. He waved to Laurel as she and her parents edged their way through the crowd. They became separated when two men loaded a bass onto the makeshift stage. Laurel arrived at Calum's table, a full minute before her parents.

"Where—did—you—get—that—stone?" Donnelly hissed, his eyes fixed on Laurel's necklace.

Laurel's long fingers curled protectively around the gray stone and she tucked the necklace inside her T-shirt.

Calum stared at his uncle, surprised by his reaction.

"Girls have all kinds of necklaces," said Tullia. "Here, honey." She handed Donnelly a ruby-colored glass. "Please excuse his voice. He's had laryngitis off and on all day."

Moments later, Rob and Andrea joined them at the table. Kenzie introduced the adults just as the lights of the bookstore dimmed. Gus stepped onto the stage and announced the first band

and the audience responded with thunderous applause.

Calum leaned closer to Laurel. "My cousins are up in the loft. Come on." As he led her upstairs, he turned back to see Donnelly staring at Laurel's retreating form.

The blue walls of the loft were complimented by a large blue-green watercolor. Several chairs and ottomans sat on a heavy braided rug. Small bookshelves and a white desk were in one corner. Two children sat on a large sofa, their feet propped on a clear blue table, peering down at the bookstore below.

"That's Brytes and Hagen," said Calum. "Will's asleep in the other room. He always gets tired on Talent Night." He nodded to Hagen. "Hagen's in our homeroom class."

Hagen smiled at Laurel.

"And Laurel's dad is the new assistant principal at Longwood," said Calum.

"Thanks a lot," muttered Laurel.

"He's gonna find out anyway." Calum motioned for her to sit with him on the sofa.

"I think I've seen Hagen before," whispered Laurel. "I don't know where, though."

"Well, duh. There's pictures of him all over my house."

Laurel sat on the sofa, her arm brushing against Hagen's.

"Ouch!" said Hagen.

"Sorry. Static electricity," said Laurel.

Calum noticed Laurel never took her eyes off Hagen as first one song, and then another played. It disturbed him that Laurel seemed to be so taken with Hagen. After a few sets, Gus returned to the stage and announced an intermission.

"LMS is a pretty big school," said Laurel, breaking the awkward silence. "How come it's so big when Emerald Lake is so small?"

"Because Longwood and Broad River are the only middle schools in Wander County," said Hagen. "All the kids from the other small towns have to go to one of them."

"It won't be as crowded next year," said Brytes.

"Why not?" asked Laurel.

"They're building a new middle school," said Brytes, looking quite full of herself. "Some students will be pulled out from Longwood, and others will come from Broad River. I'll still go to Longwood, but my class will be about two thirds the size of yours."

Hagen rolled his eyes. "If you can't guess, Brytes is well...very bright."

"That joke got old a long time ago," said Brytes. She stomped down the stairs to sit with her parents, but quickly returned saying, "Grown-ups are so boring."

An hour later, Gus' band performed the final song of the evening, Irish fiddle music that brought everyone to their feet. Rob and Andrea were saying good night when the Calum and the others joined them downstairs. They added their goodbyes, and as soon as the Werners left the bookstore, Kenzie locked the door and closed the blinds.

Books and magazines immediately sailed through the air to land gently in their proper places as the Sidhe used their talents to clean up. Dishes were sent to the dishwasher, and counters were washed by a floating spray bottle and a soapy dishrag. Ten minutes later, the two families were walking home.

Calum thought about the way Laurel had stared at Hagen, and he felt a strange anger toward his cousin. Calum was confused: why on earth was he angry with him? Hagen had done nothing. Calum shifted his focus to Laurel. She hadn't done anything either. Not really. A memory nagged him. He had felt this way before. The night Arlen had told him about Neal. Not really angry, but what? Jealous. Calum was jealous of Hagen. The revelation took Calum by surprise. He hadn't thought of Laurel as anything more than a good friend, so why should it bother him if she liked Hagen? It shouldn't. But it did.

"What do you think about Laurel?" asked Kenzie.

Calum panicked, afraid his mother had been reading his thoughts. But as the adults' conversation continued, he realized her question had been a coincidence. She wasn't talking to him.

"You were right, Kenzie," said Tullia. "There's definitely something about Laurel. But I get the feeling it's more on Rob's side than Andrea's."

Rob's side? Calum wondered. *What are they talking about?*

"Heads up," said Tullia.

Seconds later, a yellow cat darted out in front of the small group, racing across the street and into the hedges surrounding a house on the corner. A large dog barked furiously a few houses away.

Calum grinned. He'd always been impressed with Tullia's ability to make predictions. Her talent was limited, though. Her predictions came only moments in advance, but she was never wrong.

"Whatever's going on with Laurel, it's clear she doesn't know anything about that stone," said Kenzie.

"She's awfully protective of it though," said Donnelly.

"And, the stone's protective of her," said Kenzie. She explained what had happened when Kenzie had cut the necklace from Laurel's neck.

"I'd like to know how she got it," said Donnelly. "It has the Hobayeth's mark on it."

"Are you sure?" asked Kenzie.

"I think I know the mark of my own clan," Donnelly grumbled.

"And you would know if they were here? The Hobayeth?" Kenzie asked worriedly.

"Only if they wanted me to," said Donnelly.

"But you can tell Laurel's not a part of that clan, right?" asked Calum.

"Yes, I can tell. She's not Hobayeth. But that only makes things more suspicious, her having their token."

"We've been watching her for weeks. She seems to be nothing more than a normal girl," said Kenzie.

"Well, don't get too attached to her," said Donnelly. "If she's somehow figured out about us, or even a hint about our world, our next step won't be a pleasant one."

Calum glared at Donnelly and felt a shiver down his spine when he saw the look in his uncle's eyes.

Chapter Five

Sixth Grade

Calum spent the final weeks of his summer vacation hanging out with Hagen and Laurel at Siopa Leabhar. They played with Wrecks in the garden, walked to the movies, or had ice cream at Bat's while the adults had coffee and long conversations. One afternoon, as Calum and Hagen walked through the stacks, they overheard their mothers talking at the café counter.

"I think it's cute," said Tullia.

"It is," said Kenzie. "But they're growing up so fast. There was a girl we met during our last trip to South Carolina who thought Calum hung the moon."

"Hung the moon?" whispered Calum.

Hagen shrugged his shoulders.

"Of course, he was blissfully unaware of her attentions," said Kenzie. "Has Laurel said anything to him?"

Calum heard the tinkling sound of a spoon, stirring inside one of the porcelain cups.

"Not that I know of," said Tullia. "But I've seen the way she stares at him. So cute. She's the first girl to have a crush on Hagen." The shop bell rang as a customer entered the bookstore, ending their conversation.

"Wait. Laurel has a crush on me?" Hagen whispered.

Calum felt that little ball of anger again. He tried to play it off, poking Hagen in the ribs with his elbow. "Don't worry about it. I doubt Laurel has a crush on you."

"Why not?" asked a defensive Hagen.

"She doesn't think about us like that." But Calum remembered the way she had sat so close to him at the movies that day. *Or does she?*

"She sure does stare at me a lot," Hagen challenged.

"I don't know," said Calum. "Maybe she's wondering why you dress you so funny."

"Or maybe," suggested Hagen, "she's trying to figure out why someone as cool as I am hangs out with a dork like you."

"Nah," said Calum. "Must be she's trying to find out where that smell's coming from."

"Good one," said Hagen. They both roared with laughter. Their jokes continued, becoming more and more disgusting, until Tullia called Hagen to go home.

Calum's anger faded as quickly as it had come. It was stupid to think Laurel liked either one of them. He decided to put away these thoughts and appreciate Laurel for who she was. A friend who just happened to be a girl. Besides, Calum had other things to worry about.

As summer slipped away, Calum felt conflicted about middle school. He was eager to start sixth grade, but he was equally anxious. Before he could decide which emotion to follow, time made the decision for him. The first day of school arrived abruptly, like a door slamming shut on summer. He was definitely anxious.

The night before, Calum had worked his way through his school supplies. He took out his schedule card and organized his binder so each class had its own section. He filled zippered pouches with pencils, erasers, and scissors, and put them into his black book bag. His things were ready for school, but he wasn't. He didn't rest well that night, and when he did manage to fall asleep, his dreams were of lockers that closed around him like a coffin.

Kenzie and Calum stopped at Hagen's house on the first day of school before picking up Laurel. "She doesn't want to ride in with her dad," Andrea had explained. "She's worried about how the other kids will react when they find out he's the assistant principal."

As they pulled into the car line, Kenzie glanced in the rearview mirror. "Everyone okay?"

Calum half-smiled. "I guess."

"You guys are going to love middle school," said Kenzie. "And don't worry. Mr. Werner promised to keep a low profile."

Laurel smiled weakly, straightening her unmistakable first-day-of-school outfit.

"It'll be fine, really," said Kenzie. "And I hope by now, all three of you realize no one's going to be stuffed inside a locker."

Calum, Hagen, and Laurel laughed nervously and the tension was broken. They reminded each other to look for one another at lunchtime, but as Kenzie pulled up to the drop-off point, silence invaded the car like a dense fog and their collective nervousness returned.

"Okay guys," she said, bringing the car to a stop. "Have a good first day."

Calum sucked in a deep breath and opened his door. Laurel and Hagen slid out behind him wordlessly. Calum looked around the campus of Longwood Middle School and felt an intense longing for one more week of summer vacation.

The school grounds had been mowed and the smell of cut grass combined with the scent of freshly lain mulch. Small gardens with old-fashioned benches and colorful birdhouses dotted the schoolyard. Calum saw outdoor classrooms, greenhouses, and large navy barrels that were used to capture rainwater.

The car line had taken too long. By the time Calum, Hagen, and Laurel entered the school, the hallways were nearly empty. They walked across freshly waxed floors, following green signs posted on cinderblock walls. Sixth graders were to report to the Commons for an assembly. A sea of brown tables advertising school clubs made the walk deliberately roundabout—and a bit like a state fair.

SPANISH CLUB IS MUY BUENO!
THE GEOLOGY CLUB ROCKS!

Step right up and win a prize, thought Calum. A curly haired boy wearing oversized glasses handed him a brochure for the Chess Club as they walked into the Commons.

The Commons was a miniature amphitheater with stadium seating and a carpeted stage. Blue plastic chairs had been connected to form long half-circles. Calum and his friends sat in three empty seats on the back row and waited for the assembly to begin.

Calum pushed his light brown hair away from his eyes. He'd

thought he was the only one who was nervous about starting middle school, but the sound of the silent auditorium told him otherwise. Although Calum knew everyone who was coming from Longwood Elementary School, he only knew a handful of kids who came from Broad River Elementary. He searched the crowd of faces until he spotted Arlen across the Commons. Calum waved, but he couldn't get Arlen's attention.

A short man, almost as round as he was tall, walked to a tan podium on the stage. He reached up and bent the microphone until it touched his bushy gray mustache. His hair, where he still had it, was also gray.

He looks like an otter, thought Calum.

Hagen snickered.

"Good morning. I'm Mr. Taylor, principal of Longwood Middle School. Welcome to your sixth-grade year." The Otter adjusted his red-framed glasses. "This is my twentieth first day of school, and I know it will be the best one yet." The Otter spoke for a few minutes, then nodding to Mr. Werner, he said, "Please join me in welcoming our new assistant principal, Mr. Rob Werner to LMS."

Laurel's father stood and waved to the audience.

Calum glanced at Laurel, who was shifting low in her seat. The Otter continued, "Mr. Werner comes to us from a small town in Virginia. He has several…"

Calum didn't know what Mr. Werner had several of because The Otter's voice was deep and soothing and quickly lulled Calum into a daydream. He remembered what his dad had said to him the night before: "When you look back on your middle school years, you'll realize how much fun it was. Besides, you're lucky. You're going to a really nice school."

What Calum had thought was, this really nice school was about to eat him alive.

Loud applause drew him back. Mr. Taylor had finished his speech, and students were herded to the sixth-grade hall to find their homerooms. Soon hundreds of bodies jammed the hallway.

A voice called over the crowd. "Ms. Itig." It was The Otter. "Do you have a minute?"

Calum turned to get a glimpse of his homeroom teacher. She looked friendly and had short brown hair that stuck out in spikes behind her ears. Ms. Itig didn't wear glasses, at least not on her face. Instead, her glasses were on a long, beaded loop. She used them to read a card The Otter handed to her.

"Look at all these kids," Calum said gloomily. *If Finley were here, this whole middle school thing would be a lot easier. He'd be going into the seventh grade. He'd look out for us.*

"We'll get used to it," said Hagen.

They walked between rows of dull, green lockers. Each looked steely cold, and the last, number 6006, looked particularly dark and uncomfortable. Calum wondered how long he could be stuck in there before someone found him. He decided right then if that ever happened, he'd definitely use his talents to get out, no matter who saw him. As an afterthought, Calum hoped his talents would be reliable if he were in that situation. He wiped his sweaty palms on his shorts and continued down the hall, where long lines of anxious students snaked into classrooms.

Calum checked his schedule for the hundredth time, confirming his homeroom class was indeed room 611. He also had science in the same classroom, right after homeroom. Calum, Hagen, and Laurel found their way there and entered in awkward silence.

Calum was impressed by the variety of instruments, beakers, and other equipment in the room. He imagined himself at one of the lab tables, conducting a complicated experiment like a young Einstein. Looking around, he noticed a rectangular glass home for two mice. A sign on the terrarium explained their names were Lily and Lucky. A large snake skin hung on the wall near the whiteboard.

"Over here, Cal," called a voice.

Calum turned to see Arlen waving them over to his table. He introduced Laurel to Arlen, who gave her a curious look before saying, "Hey." Arlen nodded at Hagen, who responded by rolling his eyes.

Ms. Itig entered the room a few minutes later and passed out a mountain of rainbow-colored paper. "Please be sure you and your parents read these forms. Have your parents sign where indicated, and return them to me."

"I hope we don't have homework tonight," said Hagen. "It's gonna take forever just to get through all of this." He haphazardly shoved the papers into his binder.

Calum turned to Arlen and whispered, "The bus drops us off at Siopa Leabhar after school. Want to come with us?"

"Us who?" asked Arlen.

"Me, Hagen, and Laurel."

Arlen shrugged and reluctantly agreed.

The bell rang and Ms. Itig dismissed homeroom.

"Look for us at lunch," said Calum as Arlen headed to his social studies class.

Arlen nodded once before leaving the room.

Moments later, Calum, Hagen, and Laurel were separated as students were given assigned seats in alphabetical order by last name.

One seat was purposely left empty beside Calum for another student, "Who will be joining our class in a few days," explained Ms. Itig. She glanced over the card The Otter had given to her before putting it on her already cluttered desk.

"Our team meeting doesn't start for a few minutes. Let's try to get to know one another." The room was silent except for her clunking shoes. "Here's a grid with general questions. Go around the room and find people to initial the boxes. Ask as many people as you can, but don't ask someone you already know. Now's the time to make new friends."

Calum read the worksheet. The grid had statements like, "I have lived in four or more states," "I like chocolate," "I speak a foreign language," and "I have at least one pet." Calum looked around the room, no one moved.

"Well, you're going to have to get out of your seats if you want to meet anyone," said Ms. Itig. She walked over to a red-haired boy who looked like he was about to throw up. "Let's see," she said, taking the sheet from his hands. "Yes, I can initial several of these boxes." She leaned on his desk top and scribbled on the sheet. "Now that was easy enough. You guys give it a try."

Students rose slowly from their seats and moved aimlessly around the room. The red-haired boy came toward Calum. "Let's switch," he said, seeming eager to get someone's initials, other than the teacher's, on his paper.

Calum initialed the boy's grid.

"I have more than one pet, too," said the boy.

Calum relaxed a little, and in the next several minutes he had initialed five other classmates' grids.

After their ice breaker, they took a tour of the school and had their first team meeting. Calum noticed Arlen sitting with Ms. Cagle's class. Ms. Itig stood in front of the other teachers and spoke to Calum's team.

"My name is Ms. Itig," she said. "You may call me 'please Ms. Itig' or 'thank you Ms. Itig'. What I'm telling you right now goes for all of your teachers at Longwood Middle School. We have high expectations for your academic performance *and* behavior. It comes to this: if you follow the rules, we'll get along fine. If you don't, it will be a long year—*for you*. As for me, I'll be here one hundred and seventy-nine more days either way. It doesn't matter to me if you're sitting in my room or the principal's office, but if you meet our expectations then you'll have the *privilege* of remaining in our classrooms."

Calum looked at Arlen, who looked back with an "I told you so" expression.

"Stay in your seats," continued Ms. Itig, "unless you raise your hand and are given permission to move about. Do not blurt out or call out. Raise your hand, wait until you are recognized, and then you may speak. In other words, Camo Shirt"—this was directed to a boy wearing a camouflage T-shirt who had been talking while Ms. Itig laid down the law—"when I am speaking, no one else is."

During her speech, Ms. Itig made herself out to be someone with little tolerance for foolishness. But as Calum watched her more closely, he saw an entirely different person. The way her green eyes sparkled when she looked at the students, the way she brushed her hair from her face and how she glanced at the other teachers for support made her seem approachable and likeable.

The meeting lasted another fifteen minutes as the rest of the teachers introduced themselves. Calum, who had skipped breakfast, was relieved when everyone was finally dismissed for lunch. A delicious smell traveled to his nose as he opened the cafeteria door. He was thrilled to learn there would be hand-tossed pizza every day in at least one of the three serving lines.

Calum and Arlen joined Hagen and Laurel in the lunch line. "I gotta ask," Arlen said in a whisper. "What's the deal with Laurel?"

"What do you mean?" asked Calum.

"I *mean*, she's a girl."

"So?"

"So," huffed Arlen, "that was okay in elementary school, but if she hangs around with you now, people are going to think she's your girlfriend."

"Girlfriend?" Calum sputtered. "No way. She's just a friend." Laurel glanced back at Calum. She didn't appear to have heard what he'd said.

"A *friend*," said Arlen. "That's good to know."

Calum watched a sly grin sweep across Arlen's face. He intended to find out what Arlen meant by that later when they all met up at Siopa Leabhar. But Arlen didn't show that afternoon, and Calum didn't find another opportunity to ask him.

CHAPTER SIX

RILEY

The second week of school was half over when the empty chair beside Calum was at last filled by one Riley Sloan. Riley carried herself with an air of superiority and entitlement. Her name suited her because she seemed to thrive on getting everyone riled up. Her glossy red hair was bluntly cut and looked as if it had been dipped in wax. It hung in large chunks around her pale face.

Riley had eerie blue eyes, which changed suddenly with the light and looked almost black, like a dark rock pool. Her perfectly manicured nails were painted a brownish black color, which made her bone-white hands look red and angry. Riley's nose turned up slightly at the end as if she'd just smelled something rotten. Calum thought she was most likely smelling her own upper lip.

Although the new kid in a closely knit community, Riley managed to find a follower in shy Brenna Collins. The two became fast friends, isolating themselves from the rest of the class. They took turns talking about and picking on other sixth-grade students, with one exception.

Arlen.

"He's sooo cute. Don't you think?" Riley asked Brenna one

morning in science class.

"He's okay, I guess," said Brenna. "But I like Hagen. Too bad he likes Laurel. Or maybe Calum likes her. I don't know. It's weird her best friends are boys, don't you think?" Brenna flipped her mousy brown hair and rolled her insipid green eyes. "And did you notice that necklace? She wears it every single day."

"Shh. Calum's listening," said Riley. She quickly folded a strip of paper into a tight roll shaped like a small "v". When Ms. Itig turned her back to the class, Riley loaded the v-dart onto a rubber band and shot it at Calum, striking him on his arm.

Calum rubbed the point of impact and glared at Riley. For a moment he wished he could switch her schedule with John Phillip's, who was slightly less annoying. But the moment passed quickly as he wondered if that wouldn't be worse.

On Friday, the football team had their first game. Historically, sixth graders were not permitted on athletic teams, but Arlen managed to get the team manager job. He bragged to Calum about this that morning in homeroom.

"The team is awesome. The seventh and eighth-grade players rock. And since I'm the manager, I get a chance to get to know the coaches and learn all the plays. Neal's on the team, too."

"Who?" asked Calum.

"Neal. Remember? I told you about him. He was at the golf camp with me. Neal Sloan."

"Riley's brother?" asked Calum, reluctantly putting two and two together.

"Yep. Cool, huh?" asked Arlen. "And Neal's gonna be the peer helper in our PE class."

If Calum held any doubt about Arlen's new friend, it was eliminated the first day Neal worked as peer helper. Calum soon learned Neal was nothing more than a common bully. He had a knack for teasing the sixth graders whenever Coach Payne's back was turned, and Calum was his favorite target. Neal never missed an opportunity to call attention to Calum whenever he dropped the ball, missed a catch, or tripped over his own feet, especially during kickball.

"Everyone move up," said Neal. It was Calum's turn to kick. "That way you won't have to run in so far. I doubt this kid can kick it past the pitcher's mound."

Calum's nerves got the better of him and when he kicked, the ball became lodged between his feet. He barely caught himself as the ball bounced up, hitting him on his thigh.

"Way to go," Neal sneered. "You just got yourself out. Watch it, I think he's a spy for the other team," he said to the next kicker. "I swear that boy is so uncoordinated, he couldn't hit the ground if he fell down."

Riley joined her brother in making jokes about Calum's athletic abilities, saying things like "He's the best player on the other team," or "Don't stand too close to him, his skills will rub off." This backfired on her though, when Coach Payne escorted her and Calum to social studies class one day after PE.

Calum rocked back on his heels as he stood uncomfortably between his two teachers.

"Ms. Cagle," Coach Payne began, "Riley seems to be giving Calum a lot of attention. Have you seen anything like that in your class?"

"No, but you know what that usually means," said Ms. Cagle. Coach Payne gave her a meaningful look and chuckled.

What? Ugh, no way. Calum blushed deep red and cast a glance at Riley. She looked more furious than embarrassed.

Riley didn't bother Calum again. And with Hagen's help, Calum was soon able to shrug off Neal's taunts too. But what hurt Calum more than Neal teasing him was Arlen's indifference. While Arlen didn't join in with Neal, he didn't bother to put a stop to it either.

As the days passed, Arlen moved away from Calum's lunch table, choosing instead to sit by Robert Bunch, a bulky toad of a boy who sat with Riley and her gang.

While Calum's friendship with Arlen disintegrated, Calum, Hagen, and Laurel became even closer and they studied together most days after school at Siopa Leabhar. They grabbed smoothies at the café then trooped upstairs to work on homework before the influx of high schoolers arrived. With the three of them working together, their homework was easily completed, leaving them with plenty of time to hang out in the garden where Wrecks loved bouncing through the piles of autumn leaves.

Calum thought they had no secrets between them. Well, except for one important thing. The Sidhe. Maybe it was time to change that. Calum looked at Hagen one afternoon, eyebrows raised in a hopeful expression. It was weird how Hagen seemed to read his mind, before shaking his head no.

On Halloween, Ms. Itig sat at her desk to take attendance, when a loud thump made her pause. A few boys near Calum snickered, trying to suppress their laughter.

"Okay, who threw it?" asked Ms. Itig, not looking up from her computer.

One of the boys bellowed between snorts, "Ms. Itig, that shoebox was way up there." He pointed to the tall cabinets near her desk. "It jumped off your shelf and landed in your trash can." He finished the last part with a loud guffaw.

Calum looked at Hagen, as if to ask if he'd caused it.

Hagen's denial was almost negated by his stifled snicker, but Calum knew he wouldn't use his talents in such a risky way.

Ms. Itig responded to the boys' laughter as if odd things always happened in her classroom. "Hmm. I wonder if it's a mouse, or a ghost?"

Calum tried to decide if she were serious. He could never tell with Ms. Itig. *But everyone knows there's no such thing as ghosts*, he thought.

Ms. Itig instructed students to retrieve their science journals. She wrote a topic for their journal entry on the board, one that surprised Calum, because it had nothing to do with science.

Halloween is magical because…

I wonder what she's up to. Calum wrote a few sentences as Ms. Itig began her daily search for lab materials. For some reason, she had more and more trouble getting materials together as the year went on.

"It was here just a second ago," she mumbled.

When several students closed their journals, indicating they had completed the assignment, Ms. Itig stepped up her search for the next few minutes before abandoning it all together. She asked if anyone wanted to read their journal entry aloud. Susie Turnbill raised her hand, eager to share, and Ms. Itig called on her first.

"Halloween is magical because you get to be someone different." Susie was small for her age, and had platinum blonde hair that hung in thick waves down her back. She wore old and oddly matched, ill-fitting clothes, and her skin had an unhealthy hue.

Riley snorted loudly. "Yeah, maybe you'll get to be someone who has a few dollars to buy some new clothes."

Susie's best friend, Kirby Dare, cut her eyes at Riley. She slowly rose in Susie's defense, but Ms. Itig intervened. She escorted Riley from the classroom. "You'll be spending the rest of this class in Ms. Nelson's room. Please write three paragraphs on why your comment was inappropriate." Ms. Itig returned a few moments later. "I'm sorry Susie, please continue."

Susie was still pink in the face from Riley's remark, but she managed to eke out the rest of her journal entry, describing her ideas about Halloween and magic. She ended by asking Ms. Itig, "Do you believe in magic?"

"Not in the popular sense," said Ms. Itig. "I think magic is a little bit of wishing and believing, mixed with a lot of science."

Calum agreed with her. That was a fair way to describe Sidhe talents. He glanced sideways at Hagen, who looked back at him with a shrug that seemed to say, "She's close."

Calum wondered what Laurel thought about magic, and was surprised to see her staring at Hagen again. Hagen must have felt her eyes on him, because he glanced up at her. Laurel immediately averted her gaze, pretending to be distracted by a bird outside the window. Hagen seemed aggravated by this. Calum remembered their conversation at the bookstore the last week of summer.

Maybe she does have a crush on Hagen.

"So you don't believe in magic at all?" asked Susie.

"I'd have to say no. But I do believe in illusion," said Ms. Itig.

"Like a what a magician does?" asked Kirby.

"Yes," said Ms. Itig. "The good ones make it seem almost real. If the magician told you he could make a pencil float in midair, and you believed he could do it, you wouldn't look too hard for an explanation of *how* he made the pencil float. You would believe what you saw without trying to investigate the trick at all."

The dismissal bell sounded, and Ms. Itig spoke over the noise of twenty-seven students gathering their belongings. "Put your journals in the basket before you leave." She pointed to where she kept her work basket, but there was only an empty table. "Very funny. If you moved the basket for a Halloween trick, please put it back."

Not one student looked even the slightest bit guilty. Ms. Itig studied their faces until she seemed satisfied no one had purposely moved the basket. She sighed then added turn-in basket to the MOST WANTED list posted on the whiteboard.

Calum scanned the list of missing items. Erlenmeyer flask, stirring rods, triple-beam-balance. At once, Calum knew what was going on. The hard to find lab materials, the shoe box jumping off the shelf, and now Ms. Itig's missing basket could all be chalked up to one explanation.

"Trickster." Hagen confirmed Calum's theory as they filed out of the classroom.

"But how?" asked Calum. "We're the only Sidhe here."

"Apparently, we aren't."

Calum didn't believe that was possible. Surely someone, Donnelly, or even Kenzie would have known if other Sidhe were here. But Donnelly had known and had even said as much. *Dark Sidhe have come to Emerald Lake.* Calum remembered the strange storm the day he and Laurel had gone to the movies. Still, it didn't add up. Tricksters weren't necessarily evil. They just liked pulling pranks.

"Look, it's Halloween," said Hagen, interrupting Calum's thoughts. "It's the one time Sidhe run rampant through thresholds. They take advantage of everyone being distracted with costumes and trick-or-treating."

Calum was frustrated with himself for not figuring it out before. Siopa Leabhar always experienced an increase in customers from the end of October through early November. And those shoppers weren't regular tourists. Sidhe traveled to their bookstore during those weeks to search the stacks for faerie verses for the upcoming year. But while it happened every fall, Calum had never seen one of them outside of the bookstore.

"Don't worry about it. Whoever it is will clear out by the end of Halloween," said Hagen.

Calum knew Hagen was right and decided not to give it another thought.

Chapter Seven

Halloween

One of the most eagerly awaited events of Emerald Lake was the Ranson Halloween party. It had become an important gathering, divided into two distinct groups. From four until six, neighbors and a few regulars from Siopa Leabhar stopped by for heavy hors d'oeuvres of hot crab dip, black bean soup, and Beat the Devil, a spicy meat dip which was a Ranson family secret. The second wave of guests drifted in around seven thirty. These were close family friends who came to a late supper and stayed until midnight.

The Dunbar family arrived early to help set up for the party. Hagen was already dressed in his Grim Reaper costume. Calum ran upstairs, quickly dressed as a vampire, and joined the others in last-minute decorations. When he returned there was a moment of awkwardness between the two boys. Looking at each other now, Calum decided it would be the last Halloween he'd dress up like this and go trick-or-treating. He really was getting too old for these things.

"Me, too," said Hagen, giving Calum a playful punch on the arm. "Still, it's fun to wander the streets at night."

Kenzie and Tullia prepared the food using blackened cauldrons. Guests thought they were a nice touch, but these were actually treasured family heirlooms. Donnelly joked about his unique ability to decorate for the "dark" holiday, saying it was in his blood. He spoke to a spider and convinced it to spin a seriously exorbitant amount of web. Donnelly directed the webbing to various corners and doorways in each room. He tapped his fingers in the air and several pumpkins were instantly carved with detailed faces and patterns. Gus hung long black garland around the windows and fireplace, and Calum and Hagen stuffed goodie bags for trick-or-treaters. The final decorations, speakers shaped like tombstones, played eerie music throughout the house.

"Hey Dracula," said Gus. "You boys don't run off and leave Laurel behind tonight. Okay?"

"We'll keep an eye on her," said Calum.

"Be sure you do," said Donnelly, tightening the strap on Hagen's black hood. "She wears that stone for a reason."

The doorbell rang and Calum answered to find Laurel and her dad. Calum smiled at Laurel's attempt to dress like a fairy. She wore a pair of pink tights, a short silky pink skirt, and matching top. The worst part was the pair of hideous purple wings. They extended two feet above her head and flapped under their own weight when she walked by.

"My mom's idea," she hissed. "Not one word."

"Brytes is upstairs," said Hagen, suppressing a snicker. "She's gonna love your costume."

Laurel ran up the stairs, rubbing the glitter from her cheeks. "Andrea's not feeling well, and sends her regrets," said Rob. "To tell you the truth, Kenzie, I don't feel so great myself."

"Why don't you leave Laurel here with us for the night?"

Donnelly cleared his throat loudly at her suggestion.

"Thanks for the offer, but I'll swing by later to pick her up," said Rob.

"Really, it's no trouble. Calum's cousins are staying over too. If you change your mind, give us a call." Kenzie said this all too quickly, and with an unusual eagerness.

"Thanks, but Andrea will rest better with Laurel in her own bed. I'll come back at 11:30."

"That'll be fine," said Kenzie, a note of disappointment in her voice. "See you then."

Donnelly looked like he was going to explode. Kenzie had barely closed the door when he turned on her. "I thought we had an agreement," he hissed.

"Chill, Donnelly," said Gus. "I'd hate to have to kick your butt on Halloween."

"That's real funny, Gus. But if you want, we can find out later if that's even a possibility." Donnelly turned back to his cousin. "Look, Kenzie, you agreed tonight's the night. We're all going to Tusatha."

Calum's ears pricked at the word *all*. "Does he mean us, too?"

"Yes," said Gus. "Your mother and I decided it's time for you to visit the Otherworld."

"All right!" yelled Calum, giving Hagen a high five.

"Before you get too excited, you will stay by my side at all times," said Kenzie. "Understood?"

"Sure thing, Mom. Anything," said Calum. This was the opportunity he had been waiting for. A return to Tusatha, the place they had last seen Finley. Calum knew this trip would bring with it a flood of memories that would make the puzzle pieces in his mind fall into place at last. He thought this was the best night ever, until five minutes later when he answered the front door.

Arlen stood on the porch, dressed in a bloody baseball uniform. Although they had gone trick-or-treating every year since first grade, Calum was surprised to see him here tonight. It had been months since they last hung out together. Nonetheless, he felt happy to see Arlen, even if theirs was now a one-sided friendship.

"Trick or treat," said another voice, stepping from behind Arlen. It was Neal Sloan. He wore a black striped prisoner costume, complete with a ball and chain. Neal held the ball in a menacing manner, as if he were going to throw it at Calum.

Calum wanted to punch his face, but even Neal couldn't dampen his spirits, not with the news about his trip later that evening to Tusatha. Laurel came down the stairs and joined the group. She looked as surprised as Calum had been to find Arlen and Neal standing in the doorway.

"Your costumes look great," she said unconvincingly.

"Yours too," said Arlen, equally falsely.

Neal laughed. In between snorts he asked, "Are the babies going trick-or-treating with us?"

"My sister and brother," said Hagen, "have already gone out. They didn't want to scare you."

"Good one," Neal sneered.

"You guys ready then?" asked Arlen.

Calum nodded. "We're going, Mom."

"Watch for cars," Kenzie called out from the kitchen.

Calum rolled his eyes, and they all walked out into the night.

It was a cool, clear evening. The street was crowded with trick-or-treaters. Random squeals and playful screams bounced off the houses creating strange echoes throughout the neighborhood. They had only traveled one block when Neal began tormenting younger children, yelling and chasing them down the road.

"What a jerk," said Hagen.

Arlen glared at him. "At least he's trying to liven things up. Seriously, don't you think we're past too old for this?"

"Well, if that's how you feel, why don't you go back?" asked Hagen. "Or are you afraid to be in the dark all by yourself?"

"Look," said Calum, trying to diffuse the situation. "There's a haunted house at the end of the road. Let's go check it out."

The haunted house was spectacular. It was constructed of black plastic walls and a maze lead from one frightening scene to another. Calum laughed when he reached inside a plastic cauldron filled with "brains and eyeballs." Hagen and Laurel got caught in a web of glow in the dark silly string, and everyone laughed when they crashed into each other at a dead-end wall at the back of the maze. Arlen was still laughing as he stumbled out, the last to complete the maze and join the group under a streetlight on the other side of the road. They pawed through their sacks for a treat to eat on the way home.

"That was okay, I'll give you that," said Neal. "But let's go have some real fun."

"Like what?" asked Calum.

"Like this." Neal opened his trick-or-treat bag to reveal a carton of eggs. "Let's egg that house down there." He pointed to a house at the end of the road.

"They don't have their lights on," said Laurel.

"Duh," said Neal. "That's why we should egg them. I mean, who do they think they are? If they don't give out treats, they're just asking for a trick."

"They don't have their lights on because they're out of town," Calum explained.

"Perfect," said Neal. "We won't get caught."

"No, thanks," said Calum, walking away.

"Are you chicken?"

Calum turned back. "No. It's a stupid idea. Why would I want to do something like that?"

"Man, you're lame," said Neal.

"Shut up," said Hagen.

"You gonna make me?" asked Neal.

"Yeah, I can probably spare five seconds," said Hagen.

"Cut it out guys," said Laurel.

"Listen to your girlfriend," said Neal. "You don't want to get into any trouble. Her parents might not let you hang out with her anymore."

Hagen glared at Neal.

"What? It's not a secret. Is it?" Neal asked in mock innocence. "I mean the two of you."

Calum's suspicions about Laurel liking Hagen must be right if even Neal had noticed.

Laurel's cheeks flushed bright red. She strode away from the group, breaking into a run down the street toward her house.

"Does that make you feel big, picking on a girl?" Hagen challenged.

Neal flew at him, his left hand pulled back, ready to punch. Hagen's only reaction was a slight flick of his right hand. Neal tripped and landed with a thud on the leaf covered lawn.

"First day with your new feet?" Hagen grinned.

Neal stood and dusted the leaves from his costume. He studied Hagen for a long moment as if to say, "Well, let's see it then."

He knows, thought Calum. *He knows about us. But how?*

"You'd better keep away from me." Neal thrust a pointed finger at Hagen.

"No problem. I can't stand the stink," said Hagen.

Calum looked to Arlen for support but found none. His eyes were wide and filled with a curious hunger. He seemed eager to see a fight.

"Let's go, Arlen," said Neal. "There's a *real* party at Devil's Peak."

"Devil's Peak?" Calum laughed. "It's just a reserve. There's nothing there."

"There is if you know where to look," said Neal. "But some people don't see anything, not even when it's right under their nose. Come on, Arlen. Let's leave these losers."

Arlen hesitated briefly before following after Neal, who was striding purposefully down the street.

"Lapdog," Hagen smirked.

Calum quickly realized where they were headed. It couldn't

be, but yet it was. Neal was leading Arlen straight to the polder, somewhat of a train station for Sidhe. It's the gateway to any number of Sidhe mounds, dark and light.

"Wait, Arlen!" Calum called, fearful for his safety.

"Let 'em go," said Hagen.

"To the polder?"

"They're not going to the polder. They're taking a shortcut to the reserve." Hagen started back to Calum's house.

Arlen turned back to wave at Calum, before vanishing into thin air. Confused by what he had just witnessed, Calum stood frozen on the spot, straining his eyes in the darkness. Surely he had been wrong. Arlen hadn't just crossed the polder, had he?

"Come on, we need to get back before Kenzie changes her mind," said Hagen.

Calum knew he was right. His mother was probably trying to find some excuse for not going tonight. Besides, there was no way Arlen or Neal would have known about the polder. Calum ran to catch up to Hagen, and when he did Hagen took off again. The boys raced each other back to Calum's house, arriving breathless. Calum bent over, clutching a stitch in his side.

"Where's Laurel?" asked Donnelly, suddenly appearing out of thin air. Calum jumped at his uncle's voice.

"When we were close to her house, she decided to go home," said Hagen, trying to catch his breath.

"And Arlen and Neal?" asked Donnelly.

"They ditched us," said Calum, panting between words.

"Their loss," said Hagen.

"Well, you boys need to get out of those costumes. We're leaving soon," said Donnelly. "You'll look ridiculous if you go dressed like that."

Calum and Hagen quickly changed, leaving their costumes in a heap on the floor of Calum's bedroom. They bolted downstairs and waited in the kitchen, sorting their haul of candy. When the last of the guests trickled out of his house, Calum allowed his eagerness to return at the thought of going to Tusatha. His parents, aunt, and uncle joined them in the kitchen.

"Where are we going? Where *exactly*?" asked Calum.

"Public House," said Hagen. "It's where we go to Sidhe school. Hey, maybe you can go with me in December."

Kenzie busied herself at the kitchen counter, avoiding Calum's questioning eyes.

"Are you ready?" asked Donnelly.

Calum nodded. "I've been ready for a long time."

"I'll take you through this threshold to the polder so you can get the feel of going through one again," said Kenzie. She took his hand in one of hers, and Gus' in her other hand. She straightened up and led them through the threshold.

Calum felt nauseous. It was disorienting watching the layers of his kitchen peel back, revealing layers of the polder. When the peeling away stopped, he stumbled, unsteady on his feet.

Kenzie released Gus to keep Calum from falling. "Maybe that's enough for one night."

"No," said Calum. "I'm fine, Mom." He tried to shake the sensation from his head, but it only made him queasy.

"Just give him a second," Gus said gently.

The wave of nausea passed and took the dizzy spell with it. "I'm okay," said Calum. There was no way he was going to be this close and miss out on going to Tusatha. "I'm ready."

Kenzie looked doubtfully at Gus.

"He'll be fine," said Gus. "Remember how hard it was for me the first time? And I made it okay. Now it's a piece of cake." He smiled. "Let's keep going."

Kenzie took Gus' outstretched hand, and then gripped Calum's. "This time, just stare straight ahead instead of trying to keep up with the layers."

They took a few steps and without notice, the small family passed through the polder into Tusatha. It was easier this time as Calum stared directly ahead, and watched the layers fly away in his peripheral vision. With each layer tearing off, the polder revealed a new section of the Otherworld. Soon Tusatha came fully into view. The sights and smells of the Otherworld were cleaner, more pronounced. The evergreens were greener, the autumn colors more colorful. The air was crisp and fresh, like winter's first snowfall. When none of the polder was left, Calum found himself on the side of a gentle hill covered in sweet-smelling emerald-green grass. Hagen and his family followed a few moments behind them.

"Better?" asked Gus.

"Yeah. Looking ahead worked." The dizziness was mild this time and there was no nausea. Calum stared at the landscape, straining to recognize something, anything familiar. But no memories came to him.

"You can't force it," said Kenzie. "Just relax and enjoy being here for now."

Disappointed but still hopeful, Calum walked with the others down a wide dusty path toward the center of the mound. A large banner hung across the street which read, "WELCOME TO TUSATHA." Something like glitter fell from the banner when they walked beneath it. It felt cool and pleasant on Calum's face, and when he stuck out his tongue, it tasted like honey. He smiled, happy to be back in his element. He stood with his parents and surveyed Tusatha Mound. Colorful tents were clustered on smooth meadows, showcasing the traditions and specialty foods of different Sidhe clans.

"Come on, Hagen," said Tullia. "Let's go find your grandparents."

"Okay if I stay with Calum?" asked Hagen. "Just for a while?"

"It's fine with me," said Kenzie.

"We'll catch up later," said Donnelly, ruffling Hagen's hair. He led Tullia further into the crowd.

Calum listened as Kenzie explained what each of the clans offered inside their tent. It took him only a moment to decide where he wanted to go first. The Foletti. The ancient artifacts of the Italian clan fascinated him. He poured over several scrolls of Italian writing, sipping on a cup of their wonderfully strong coffee. Kenzie had added nearly the same amount of cream before giving the cup to Calum, but he still thought it was the best drink he'd ever tasted. After Kenzie promised to take him to the Foletti Mound another day, Calum reluctantly agreed to leave their tent.

Next, they stopped to sample smooth German chocolate at the Weisse Frau tent. They stayed for a few minutes, listening to a beautiful waltz, but Calum was ready to move on when his parents began twirling on the dance floor. The next tent belonged to the African, Abatta clan. Calum found their vibrant paintings and sculptures interesting, but their prophetic poetry was a bit over his head.

When they entered the slick black tent of the Kischef clan, Calum felt a strange sense of déjà vu. A haze of heavy incense filled the air, triggering a memory inside him. "I know these things," he said, sorting through a wooden bin of velvety gray crystals.

"May I help you?" asked a tall blonde-haired woman behind the back counter. She was easily six feet tall and had a slight build. She crossed the space between them quickly, gracefully, in a fluid motion.

"We're friends with Rebeccah," said Kenzie. "Is she here?"

The woman cackled loudly, showing a mouthful of crooked teeth. This startled Calum, but he couldn't pull himself away from her mesmerizing gaze. She began to turn on the spot, spinning faster and faster until she was a blur. When she stopped spinning, she looked entirely different. The woman was now every bit of five feet tall. She had black wiry hair and her eyes were black as night. She approached them more slowly this time, walking with a slight limp.

"Trick or treat," said the woman. "It's good to see you MecKenzie, and Gus too." She hugged them both.

"It's good to see you again Rebeccah," said Kenzie.

"And this young man, he is my treat?" A white-faced Calum stared blankly, unable to speak. "This can't be Calum," said Rebeccah. "He was a baby last time I saw him. Let me have a look, mein freid." Her boney hands rested on Calum's shoulders as she looked him over.

"Mein freid?" asked Calum. He couldn't remember much about Rebeccah, but he knew she was someone he'd once liked very much. He immediately trusted this stranger, and was glad to see her again.

"It's Yiddish. It means my delight," said Kenzie. "Rebeccah used to call me that."

"You are still my delight, MecKenzie," said Rebeccah. "It's so good to see all of you. How was your trip in?"

"Calum had a little trouble," said Kenzie.

"It will pass, with practice." Rebeccah smiled. "And here's my other young friend. Hello Hagen." She pulled him into a tight hug.

"Hey Rebeccah," said Hagen, squirming.

"Such a handsome young man, just like his dad."

Hagen blushed and tried to pull away, but there was no use. Rebeccah was in charge of all of her hugs.

"Is it okay if I take Calum to Public House now?" Hagen asked when Rebeccah finally let go of him.

Kenzie looked nervously at Gus.

"He's perfectly safe here," Gus said reassuringly.

"He's right," said Rebeccah. "There's nothing to worry about."

Kenzie smiled and gave Hagen a nod.

"Come on. All the kids get to have Ghoul Gruel," said Hagen. "It's not as bad as it sounds. It tastes like chicken soup."

"You must come visit me when you come back for Sidhe

school, yes?" Rebeccah called after them.

Calum smiled. "Definitely." He turned and followed Hagen out of the tent. They quickly walked to the northern most part of the mound. The street was lined with various small shops, each spilling party goers onto the sidewalk. The road came to an end at the front steps of the Tusatha Public House.

The building had deep cherry-colored shake siding with intricate markings on its supports and around each window. The multi-angled roof had similarly colored wooden shingles. The house was decorated in autumn colors of brown, gold, and burnt orange. Fat batches of yellow mums lined the front porch.

Calum followed Hagen up the front steps and inside the house. The front hall was lined with heavy oak panels, each covered with mysterious carvings—Gaelic writing—similar to the writing on the checkout desk at Siopa Leabhar.

"What's all this?" Calum fingered the neatly written text of one panel.

"Our stories," said Hagen. "Every Sidhe's story is carved into the entrance hall of their Public House. See, mine's down here." He pointed to where his name was neatly carved on the base of one of the planks. "Good looking, intelligent, first born child of Tullia and Donnelly Dunbar."

"Right," said Calum, easily reading what was written on the plank.

"You have one, too," said Hagen. "In the Aessea Public House." They continued down the hall, Hagen pointing out the names of his relatives. "Here's Tullia, and that's Brytes over there."

"And here's Finley's," said Calum, gently touching the carv-

91

ing. Finley's story was short, even shorter than Brytes'.

Hagen nudged him and they continued through the hall. Interconnected wooden circles gleamed in the floor at the end of the entrance hall, leading to a large room called "The Circle." Mums and acorn centerpieces sat on tables that lined the edges of the massive room, where families enjoyed specialty foods from the tents. The open space on the floor was covered with large fluffy cushions. They walked to a table loaded with Sidhe treats and filled their plates with broken broomsticks, butterfly shadows, and willow whips. They picked up a glass of Swamp Swill and found an empty space where they could sit together on the floor.

A rough-skinned hobgoblin sat on a three-legged stool. He held a cloud cake in one hand and tore crooked bites with his large gray teeth. The hobgoblin barely chewed the food before washing it down with gulps of a frothy drink. He belched with a rumbling roar.

"Now as you already know, the duine daonna are not that great at trudgin' through the woods," said the hobgoblin.

Hagen and a few other kids snickered.

Calum was sure Hagen had heard the tales for years, and could probably recite them from memory. But Calum decided he wasn't going to miss a thing. He settled on a soft cushion with his Swamp Swill and listened to the hobgoblin's *Tales from a Will o' the Wisp*, feeling he was home at last.

CHAPTER EIGHT

TUSATHA

October faded into November, and Thanksgiving break soon arrived. Calum and his parents spent most of the holiday discussing the upcoming Sidhe school session in December.

After much convincing and promises to stick with Hagen, Kenzie relented. Calum would be allowed to return to the Otherworld over the Christmas holiday. There was one small problem. Laurel. Calum hated lying, but he had no choice. He decided to tell her he was going to spend Christmas with his grandparents in South Carolina.

Christmas break couldn't come fast enough. After Neal's taunting on Halloween, Hagen had become increasingly irritated with Laurel's apparent affections. He reached his limit during the first week of December when Laurel was absent from school with the flu. Mrs. Werner asked Calum to bring Laurel's assignments home. When Kenzie pulled into Laurel's driveway, Hagen refused to get out of the car.

"It's okay if I don't see her for one day," said Hagen. "I *think* she'll live."

Kenzie turned around in her seat, looking at Hagen with

raised eyebrows. Calum left in a hurry before Hagen got the lecture that would surely follow.

Calum knocked at the door and was greeted by Mrs. Werner and Whisper. The black-and-white cat followed Calum through the house, eyeing him suspiciously when he set Laurel's binder on the kitchen table.

"Thanks for bringing her work," said Mrs. Werner. "Laurel's not up to visitors, but she'd probably like it if you'd message her later."

"I will. I hope she feels better."

Calum returned to the car in time to hear his mom saying, "I'm sure Laurel just has a harmless crush on you. Try to be patient, Hagen. She'll get over it. Until then, be nice to her. And no matter what, it's never okay to talk to me in that tone."

"Sorry, Kenzie," said Hagen, looking angrier than Calum had ever seen him.

Calum thought something else might be bugging Hagen. Since Arlen was out of the picture, maybe Hagen wanted to drive Laurel away, too? Over the next couple of days, Hagen continued to be short with Laurel, which caused Calum to be short with Hagen. Calum took it upon himself one afternoon at Siopa Leabhar to clear the air with his cousin.

"I think of you as the brother I never had," said Calum. "You and I are way closer than two friends could ever be. Laurel will never take your place."

"Gee thanks, you big dork. I'm sure I feel flattered." Hagen laughed. "I *love* you, too," he said between snorts. "Look, every-thing will be all right if Laurel would just stop staring at me all the time. People are starting to say things and I don't just mean Neal. Wait, he's not a person. He's more of a troll."

Unfortunately for Calum, things continued to be strained whenever the three friends were together. Both Hagen and Laurel now looked for excuses not to be around the other. The three still studied at Siopa Leabhar after school, but even that changed to accommodate their unpleasant moods. By an unspoken agreement, Hagen and Laurel took turns working with Calum in the loft. Whenever one was with Calum, the other worked on their assignments in the coffee bar below.

The week before Christmas seemed to last an eternity. Everyone, students and teachers alike, needed a break from school, homework, and from each other. Parents, however, looked forward to going to Longwood for the first orchestra concert of the year. The concert was scheduled for the evening before Christmas break.

Calum had become quite good with his violin, but he was still a bundle of nerves when he arrived with his parents for the concert. They made their way to the Commons, Calum taking each step like a condemned man.

"Relax," said Kenzie. "You've played lots of times at Siopa. You'll be great."

"And I'll be on the stage with you." Gus clapped him on his back.

"Why?" asked Calum.

"The bass player is sick. Ms. Rathbone just asked me to sit in."

Great. Calum smiled weakly.

"I see Tullia and Donnelly sitting with the Werners." Kenzie casually waved at them.

Why did Laurel have to come? Calum wondered. *What if I mess up?* He watched Hagen climb the steps to the stage. Halfway up, his viola slipped from hands and tumbled down the steps. It seemed Calum wasn't the only one who was nervous.

"Break a leg, you guys." Kenzie gave Gus a quick peck on the cheek and joined Tullia in the audience.

"I'll break yours if you break mine," Calum muttered to Gus, who shook his head. Calum half-wished he would break a leg to get out of performing. He joined the rest of his classmates on stage, wiping his sweaty hands on his pants. *I'll never be able to hold onto my bow.* But Calum felt a little better once they started playing and his confidence quickly grew.

Ms. Rathbone addressed the audience after their third piece. "Parents, please raise your hand if you do *not* know how to play an instrument." Several hands shot into the air. "My students are quite gifted. So talented they can teach anyone to play. May I please have a few volunteers?" A small group of parents ambled forward. Calum was mortified to see Kenzie among them.

"A few of my maestros will take you backstage and teach you an easy little song while the rest of the orchestra plays our final piece." Several seventh-grade students led the parents offstage. "We can't wait to hear your performance."

"This should be good," said Calum. "The only thing Kenzie can play is her iPod."

As the orchestra finished a slow sonata, the adult "students" joined them onstage. Ms. Rathbone conducted as the parents played a ridiculously funny version of *Mary Had a Little Lamb*.

Calum felt ten times better once he heard how horrible they sounded. He didn't mind at all when Ms. Rathbone again asked for volunteers to join the orchestra for a special encore. Calum smiled as he watched teachers, parents, and Kenzie dance while the orchestra played the *cancan*.

After the concert, Laurel joined Calum and Hagen on stage. "That was great." She looked at Hagen shyly while she dragged her pendant across its velvet cord. The cord snapped and the pendant fell to the floor.

Hagen bent to retrieve it at the same time as Laurel, almost bumping heads. She snatched the pendant away before Hagen touched it. Maybe the stress of the evening had finally caught up with him, or maybe it was the anticipation of going to Tusatha. Whatever the reason, Hagen had reached his breaking point.

"Sorry. I was just trying to pick it up for you," he said gruffly. "By the way, do you have to stare at me *all the time*? It really was distracting during the concert."

Several students stopped packing their instruments, curious about Hagen's comments.

"Cool it," whispered Calum.

"Seriously Laurel," Hagen continued, unaware of his audience. "What gives? Can you try staring at someone else for a change?"

Laurel struggled to speak; a muffled cry escaped her lips before she ran off the stage and into the crowd. Her parents ran after her.

"Not cool," said Donnelly, climbing on to the stage. "I think you could have picked a better time and place."

"Or, maybe not said anything at all," said Tullia, joining

them.

"Okay," said Hagen. "I get it."

Tullia lifted one eyebrow and stared at him. "I'd think long and hard about what you say next."

"And, how you say it," said Donnelly.

When Kenzie ushered Calum off the stage to help Gus pack up the bass, he didn't protest. Calum glanced back in time to see Hagen nodding to whatever Donnelly was telling him. He wondered if things would ever get back to normal for him, Hagen, and Laurel. He hoped the long Christmas break apart would do the trick.

𝒲𝒾

Calum and his parents always spent Christmas Day together at home. When Calum and Wrecks trotted downstairs that morning, they found Kenzie and Gus waiting in the family room. The curtains had been pulled back, revealing the beautiful mountain side, which was covered in a thick blanket of fresh snow.

"Merry Christmas," Calum said excitedly.

"Merry Christmas." His parents echoed. They motioned him to join them on the couch where they all enjoyed their traditional Christmas breakfast of soft-boiled eggs on thick toast. Just when Calum could wait no more, Gus said, "Go ahead, son."

Calum dove under the tree, and with Wrecks' help, passed out all the Christmas presents. Calum was surprised to discover a silver watch on a leather strap among his gifts. Calum read the inscription, "My son, my spirit."

"Your granddad gave me that watch when I started middle school," said Gus. "I had to replace the strap, but the watch still works."

"It's cool. Thanks Dad." Calum was thrilled to have something his father had when he was a kid. He sat beside Gus for several minutes, one hand on his dad's shoulder and the other turning the watch over and over, looking at it from all angles.

After tidying up the ripped wrapping paper and torn ribbons, Calum jogged up the stairs to pack for his trip to Tusatha. He overheard his parents' conversation.

"That was the best gift ever," said Gus.

"What?" asked Kenzie.

"Just being here with Calum."

"Yeah, he won't do that much longer. Before we know it, he'll be spending more and more time with his friends," said Kenzie.

I'll always want to spend time with you guys, thought Calum.

Since Kenzie's parents were visiting friends in Aessea and would not return to Tusatha until the end of the school session, Calum would be staying with Hagen's grandparents, Connor and Aine Brady, the King and Queen of the Faerie Realm. This eased Kenzie's worries enough to permit Calum to travel with Hagen without her. The boys passed through the thresholds with ease the day they returned to Tusatha.

The Public House had been painstakingly decorated for the Christmas season. A large, live tree stood growing in the center of the room. It was adorned in different shades of cream. There were hundreds of delicate ivory-colored ornaments, which depicted various winter scenes. Small ceramic shapes in pale white shades were scattered about the tree. A large cream-colored bow was perched on the top, its ribbons gracefully trailing downward on two sides of the tree. Aside from the sheer size and the multitude of ornaments, this tree was special in another way. Every few minutes a gold shimmering began at the top of the tree and worked its way to the ground. As the shimmering passed through each branch, the decorations changed color. This time they changed to different shades of robin's egg blue, but in another ten minutes they would all be shades of lilac.

A booming voice called out, "Hello Calum! So good to see you again. And you too, Hagen."

"Hello, Father." Hagen waved to Father Christmas, who was surrounded by small Sidhe. Hagen led Calum up a flight of stairs. "You probably forgot where everything is, so I'm going to show you around." He pointed to a room on the right side of a long hallway. "This is kinda like a playroom. But we learned our first talent here. We were three years old. Remember it?"

Calum peered through the door's window. It was an oversized sitting room with dozens of comfortable-looking chairs, blankets, and cushions. Thick carpets covered bamboo floors and a fireplace hovered in a corner, far out of the reach of curious toddlers. Calum breathed in a buttery, vanilla scent. "*Accessi*," he whispered.

"That's right." Hagen clapped him on the back. "I knew you'd remember."

"But how?" asked Calum.

"The smell. Talents are linked to specific scents. It helps us remember how to do the magic. Or remember not to do it," said Hagen. "Scents linked to dark magic smell horrible, like rotten eggs. It's like a punishment for using dark magic."

"That kind of punishment doesn't sound too bad," said Calum. "I mean, it doesn't really stop anyone from doing dark magic. Does it?"

"Well it's not like the Rule of Seven, that's for sure."

"The what?" asked Calum.

Hagen looked at him. "Kenzie never intended for you to come back here, did she?"

Calum hadn't considered that, but he supposed Hagen was right. If Kenzie had wanted Calum to return, surely she would have told him these things. "I guess not."

They walked further down the hall. "The Rule of Seven is…sort of like a time out, or being grounded," he said. "It works like this: little kids get seven minutes, elementary kids seven hours, middle schoolers seven days, and high schoolers seven weeks."

"Seven weeks seems like a long time to be grounded," said Calum.

"Most of us learn fast," said Hagen.

"Most?"

"Some never learn. And adult Sidhe have other punishments."

"Like?" prompted Calum.

"Banishment. Adult Sidhe who use dark magic are banished for seven months. If they do something really bad, they can be banished for seven years, or even seven lifetimes. Which really means they're out for good."

"So, what's with all the sevens?" asked Calum.

"Seven's important in nature," said Hagen. "There are Seven

Seas, Seven Climes, and Seven Steps of Alchemy. Even a tabby cat has seven stripes going down the back of its head." He led Calum up another flight of stairs.

A woody smell permeated the air. Calum breathed deeply. "Baby pine."

"Yeah, it's the Nature Room. We moved here when we were five. We learned how to find water, make our way through the woods, and identify animals, trees, and lots of other things about being in a forest in the Realm of Man. It's the last room you were in before you stopped coming."

When they climbed to Level Three, they were greeted by a horrid stench. "Ugh, where are we now?" asked Calum.

"The Reason Room. This room is for eight-year-olds…" said Hagen, "…the age of accountability. It's where we learn about right and wrong—you know, dark magic."

"How do you stand it?" His eyes watered and he pinched his nose to stop the smell. Calum started up the next flight of stairs without waiting for Hagen's lead.

"It doesn't smell bad to me. When you make the right choice, the scent changes to something really good, and it's a scent that's different for everyone. After that, you only smell the disgusting ones when you make the wrong choices when using your talents." They had reached the top of the stairs. "This is Level Four, the last level. I moved here when I turned twelve. We'll stay at this level until we turn fifteen. Our classes are in here."

"Classes? How many?" asked Calum.

"Two. I've already been through the first one: the Intentions Room. It's where we learn how to gather intentions of those around us." He put his fingertips to his temples and pretended to meditate. "Supposed to protect us from dark magic," he said in a scary voice.

"Very funny," said Calum. "You said there were two. What's the other?"

"The Astronomy Room."

Calum sniffed but could not make out a scent.

"Yeah, I don't smell it either. We don't get this one until we complete the fourth level."

While Hagen was an average student in the Realm of Man, he was one of the top students in the Tusatha Public House. He was gifted at gathering intentions, and was also quite good at listening to the messages of trees.

Calum, on the other hand, turned out to be a strong student in both realms. He was good at memorizing facts, images, and even the smallest details of conversations. This was a skill that came in handy when he began to study Sidhe history. He could recite the names of all of the clans and knew their obscure traditions. Kenzie, who never remembered a thing, believed this ability skipped a generation because her father never forgot anything, no matter how inconsequential.

Their time at Sidhe School was brief, so their days were long. Calum squirmed in his wooden seat, trying to find a comfortable position as his school day ticked into the eighth hour. He looked around the classroom for a distraction from the seemingly never-ending lecture on astronomy. Telescopes lined the only wall that was free of floor-to-ceiling bookshelves. Celestial charts had been pulled down, covering the blackboard.

"Psst," said Hagen. "Do you want to go to the Kischef Bergele after class to see Rebeccah?"

Calum nodded, eager to see her again. Besides, he could use a break from the hazing of his Sidhe classmates. When they realized Calum was a new student, they took pleasure in introducing themselves. Calum didn't mind making new friends, but first contact between Sidhe children resulted in a mild electrical shock, similar to the shock Calum felt from static electricity. He soon found the anticipation of the shock was worse than the actual sting.

"And what do you make of it, Hagen?" asked Twicely. Twicely Keane was Calum and Hagen's astronomy teacher. Her family was known for a long history of twin births. Twicely earned her unusual name because she was the second child born in her family without a twin. She paced the front of the room, waiting for Hagen to answer.

"What's she talking about?" asked Hagen. But he didn't actually *say* anything.

Calum's ears perked. *I heard that.*

Good for you, thought Hagen. *So what's she talking about?*

"I'm talking about Pluto," said Twicely, pointing to the small planet on one of the charts.

"Oh, yeah," said Hagen. "The duine daonna don't get it because they can't stop arguing about whether or not Pluto is a planet. They don't understand it belongs to an entirely different universe. Our universe."

Calum stared at him, trying frantically to read more thoughts, but his mind hit a blank wall.

"Relax Calum," said Twicely. "That's how it works. You'll pick up random thoughts, and then sometimes go for days without hearing any. When you come back at the end of summer, you'll learn about blocking thoughts. Or as we call it, shutting the door of your mind. Until then, and even after," she said, looking from Calum to Hagen, "you both need to pay attention in class."

"Sorry Twicely," said Calum.

She smiled at him briefly before continuing her lecture on the planets that are shared by the Realm of Man and the Otherworld.

Calum enjoyed his time in Tusatha, but he counted the minutes until the end of class, eager for his visit to Kischef Mound. School is still school in any realm. When they were finally released, Calum and Hagen walked to the polder just outside Tusatha. No longer having any negative reactions to traveling through thresholds, Calum walked deliberately and without hesitation through the polder to the Kischef Mound.

Kischef was a centuries-old mound, and a favorite shopping place of all Sidhe clans. Sunlight bounced over copper-covered roof tops of the quaint houses below. Wisps of smoke rose from each circular shaped chimney, and wooden carts bursting with a variety of items for sale clogged both sides of the road. The streets were leathery paths, and on this day they were filled with people.

Hagen turned off the main road onto Argentinische Allee. "It's down there," he said, pointing to a shop at the end of the road. "The Four Corners."

The shop was remarkably small considering the variety of crystals and gemstones sold there. Hundreds of bins of colorful crystals crowded wooden tables. These rocks and minerals were special, having been grown in the cave gardens of Avalon. The entire space smelled of spearmint tea, and Calum's stomach growled when his eyes found a plate of chocolate covered croissants.

"Mein freid, Calum," said Rebeccah, wrapping her arms around him. "And Hagen. What a pleasant surprise." She gave Hagen a quick hug hello. "This must be my lucky day. It's good to see you both. You boys look hungry. The pastries are for eating. Help yourselves."

Hagen already had. His pastry was nearly gone when he managed one word between mouthfuls. "Good."

Calum reached for a pastry and quickly took a bite. Dark chocolate flooded his mouth. "These *are* good."

A young woman entered the store and waited by the front counter.

"Excuse me for one second," said Rebeccah. "Coming."

"Let me show you some stuff," said Hagen. He led Calum deeper into the shop, pointing out different stones and vials of faerie dust. "This one makes your enemy forget they are your enemy. The forgetfulness only lasts about ten minutes, but it's long enough you could get away." He set the vial down, and Calum picked up another.

"Mom's got this one at Siopa. It's a calming dust," said Calum.

"Right," said Hagen.

Calum replaced the vial and allowed his hands to glide over cool velvety crystals in a nearby bin. These were the same crystals he had noticed during his Halloween visit to Tusatha.

"Ulexite," said Rebeccah, returning to the boys near the back of the store. "It helps with decision making. A bonus is its disinfecting properties. I think you should have this one." She slipped a corded ulexite pendant over Calum's head. "Here are the instructions for the stone's care. So, how is school going?"

"It's hard, but fun," said Calum. He could hardly believe he'd actually used the word "fun" to describe school. "School here is different to school in the Realm of Man."

"As are your classmates, I'd guess," said Rebeccah. "Meet many friends here yet?"

"A few," said Calum. For some reason, he thought about Laurel. It was strange, but he actually missed her.

"And who is Laurel?" asked Rebeccah.

Calum sighed. *Did everyone have to hear his thoughts?*

"She's a friend of ours, mine and Hagen's," said Calum. "I don't know if you'll be able to meet her though, she's duine daonna."

"No faerie blood, eh?" asked Rebeccah.

"No. And she doesn't know about us," said Hagen.

"Yet," said Calum.

Hagen raised one eyebrow and stared at Calum. "Ever."

"If you're thinking of telling her, she must be special," said Rebeccah. "And if she's special, I must meet her. If you do tell her, bring her by sometime."

"I don't think I can," said Calum. "I mean, I don't think my talents are strong enough to bring her through a threshold."

"I have just the thing," said Rebeccah slyly. She opened the only drawer in a circular table and pulled out a silver ring. "We'll call it years of missed birthday and Christmas gifts."

Calum slipped the ring on a finger on his right hand. It had an oval-shaped blue sapphire set horizontally inside a thin black line of jet.

Rebeccah took Calum's hand. "This is a travelon. It allows for one co-traveler between the worlds. *Adstringo*," she murmured. "It will protect the duine daonna as if she were one of us."

"Cool. Thanks, Rebeccah," said Calum.

"As for you, Hagen," said Rebeccah. "A seasoned traveler. I've got just the gift." She led them to the front of the store and handed Hagen two stones. "Beryl and kyanite, two good journey stones. Carry the beryl for two days prior to your departure, but leave the beryl behind and take the kyanite on your journey."

"Thanks Rebeccah," said Hagen. A bell tolled from the Kischef Public House. "It's getting late, we'd better get back."

"I need to pay for the ulexite," said Calum. "Mom only gave me one coin. I hope it's enough."

Hagen laughed. "It's plenty. I'll show you." He led Calum to the checkout counter, and took the small gold coin from Calum. "This is a Bart. We get one on our eighth birthday. The back has our clan's mark and the front has our Barter." He pointed to an image of an old man with a long beard and square shaped spectacles. "That's Rebeccah's Bart." He put Calum's coin on the counter next to hers. The images on the faces of both coins came to life and they began to haggle over the price of the items. "When they agree on a price, that amount of money moves from your account to Rebeccah's."

The images shook hands and returned to still life on their coins.

"Cool," said Calum. He picked up the Bart and stared at it with a newfound appreciation.

"Thanks, boys," said Rebeccah. She wrapped Hagen's touchstones in moss-green paper and tied the package with a brown cord. "And please, not so much time between visits, yes?"

"No problem," said Calum. His eyes roamed the store once more. He wondered if Kenzie would let him work at The Four Corners next summer, instead of Siopa Leabhar.

"Let me know what she says," said Rebeccah, waving goodbye.

Wi

Calum's grandparents, Uilleam and Salena Lindsey, were due back at Tusatha on the last day of class. Calum ran all the way to their house after school that day. He smiled as the scent of vanilla pipe tobacco washed over him when he opened the door. His grandfather's pipe.

Calum found his grandparents in the kitchen. Neither of them had a trace of gray hair. Uilleam was tall and carried himself in a dignified manner, even in the most casual surroundings. Salena was petite, but strong. Her face lit up when Calum approached.

"Uilleam, Salena, I've missed you," said Calum, throwing himself into his grandfather's waiting arms.

"Good afternoon," said Uilleam. "How was school?"

Before Calum could answer, he was pulled away into a tighter embrace. "You're growing too fast, and you feel thin. Are you eating enough?" asked Salena.

"Uh, Uilleam," said Calum, struggling to catch a breath. "If you're not busy, could I talk to you outside?"

Salena drew back and smiled at Calum. "Asking advice about girls?" She pinched his cheek.

"Leave the boy be," said Uilleam. "Good heavens, he's not a baby anymore."

Salena released Calum. "Don't be long, supper's almost ready."

Uilleam sighed. "We'll be back in a few minutes." He led Calum outside and down the path to the garden. A golden light shimmered and danced between several wooden posts in the ground. "Sprites," he said. "They can't resist post racing. It amazes me duine daonna don't notice sprites running through their highway guard rails."

Calum looked closer and saw two small sprites racing between the evenly spaced posts.

"Uilleam, I was wondering, do you know anything more about Finley?" Calum looked up into his grandfather's face. *Will I ever be that tall?*

Uilleam sighed and smiled softly at Calum. "I have no news, but Connor and I haven't stopped looking. Finley has to be somewhere. We will find him."

They sat on a wooden bench in front of a small pond. Calum threw stones into the water and watched the ripples roll across the surface. "I was wondering, is there any way Finley could be an Addition?"

"That's very unlikely. Even when it was common practice for Sidhe to add duine daonna to their clans, it was never acceptable for faeries to kidnap other faeries. It did happen once though. They caught the faerie responsible and applied the Rule of Seven. He was banished to the Void for seven lifetimes."

Calum had heard of the Void. A place caught between the Otherworld and the Realm of Man. It was a place of nothingness, loneliness, and despair. Calum shuddered, thinking about what it must be like, forced to live there. "When did that happen?" he asked.

"That Addition occurred before your mother was born, and no one else has dared to try it again. If that's what happened to Finley, the punishment will be none the less." Uilleam put an arm around his grandson's shoulders. "Child, please stop blaming yourself for what happened to Finley. You don't need forgiveness. You need acceptance. Guilt and worry are twin brothers to regret, and all three are terrible wasters of time."

"It's just that Kenzie never says anything about him."

"I think it's easier for her not to talk about it. Your mother has a bit of trouble separating guilt from acceptance, too. But if you want to talk, you can always call for me and I will be right there."

A memory of Kenzie's face appeared in Calum's head. He could hear her frantic screams for Finley as she searched the house, the yard, everywhere for him. A pain of longing shot through Calum. He was ready to go home.

CHAPTER NINE

NIGHT SCHOOL

Calum returned to Emerald Lake on the last day of Christmas break. He stayed up late with Kenzie and Gus, sharing every detail of his time at Sidhe school. He had worried about how Kenzie would react to his visit to Rebeccah's shop and the ring she had given him, but it didn't seem to bother her at all. In fact, she seemed happy about the ring because of the, "added protection when you travel."

Calum's workload doubled when school started back at LMS. January passed quickly and February froze in. The teachers at Longwood sensed the annual bog-down of their students and decided it was time for Night School.

Each grade celebrated Night School on a different evening. It was a time when the school was open for students to come in and enjoy various games, activities, or watch a movie. The Multipurpose Room was the place to go for scooter races. There was Cafeteria Karaoke, ping pong tournaments against the teachers, and games of Horse in the gym.

Things were still strained between Hagen and Laurel, but Calum was happy they both agreed to come to Night School, even though they sat on opposite ends of the aisle during *Napoleon Dynamite*. They watched the movie in the Commons with Kirby Dare, Susie Turnbill, and Barry Langley. It was the second viewing of the DVD that evening, and they were the only ones who stayed to watch it again. This was one of their favorite movies. They knew all the lines, which made for an interactive experience.

"Your mom went to college," quoted Barry.

"Yes, she did," agreed Calum, and they all burst out laughing.

"Why don't you make me some que-see-dee-ahs?" asked Hagen.

"Make your own dang que-see-dee-ahs," said Kirby evoking more laughter.

"Oh, look," Riley sneered in her sickening sugary voice. She stood behind the rows of chairs, which had been lined up theater-style for the movie. "They're taking notes on how to be cool."

"I wouldn't follow their lead," jeered a boy's voice as he motioned to the large video screen.

Arlen Stanton.

"That makes one person you wouldn't follow," Calum said before turning his back on his former friend.

"Ouch," said Hagen.

"Ignore them and they'll go away," Laurel whispered to Calum.

"Why would we do that?" asked Riley. "We'd love to join your little group." When no one responded, Riley continued. "Come on, if you don't play along, it's not as much fun."

"I think it's interesting that with all of the things you could be doing right now, you choose to watch us. Tell me, Riley, are we that fascinating to you? Should we feel flattered?" asked Laurel.

Riley stormed off in a huff, closely followed by Brenna and Arlen. Calum and his friends were not bothered by them for the rest of the evening.

Night School was exactly what the sixth graders needed to recharge their batteries. They seemed to be shaking off the winter doldrums when they returned on Monday morning. Calum, Hagen, and Laurel were in a happy mood until they reached the sixth-grade hallway.

By this point in the school year, Calum and his classmates were able to get in and out of their lockers within a few minutes. Books were still dropped and accidentally kicked down the hall, or someone would forget about the locker door above their own and bump their head as they stood up, but it was an organized chaos. Students managed to get around each other quickly to retrieve their morning books and materials. That morning, however, the students stood bewildered, frozen in front of their lockers. Teachers wandered between them, trying to discover the cause of the unusual quiet.

"What in the world?" asked Ms. Itig. "Who's responsible for this?"

Calum heard other teachers asking similar questions, but no one seemed to have an answer.

The padlock on every locker had been flipped so the dial was now facing the locker door. There was no way to access the combination. It was a long wait while each lock was individually opened with a master key.

Riley showed up late as usual. "I wonder what happened

here?" she asked Brenna, who giggled wildly.

"Cute, Riley," said Laurel. "It's just like you to be such an inconsiderate brat."

"Ms. Itig," Riley said loudly. "I wonder how anyone could have done this without a key."

"What are you talking about?" asked Ms. Itig, eyeing her with a mixture of frustration and suspicion.

"You know, one of those master keys like the ones the principals have." She looked directly at Laurel. "Or someone close to the principal."

Laurel's face and neck turned beet red.

"If you have something to say, say it," demanded Calum.

"Oh, I think actions speak louder than words, don't you?" asked Riley.

"Calum, do you know anything about this?" asked Ms. Itig. She was joined by another science teacher Calum recognized as Mr. Craven.

Calum felt as if he were roasting on a pit. His throat dried and he coughed out an unconvincing "no."

Ms. Itig's eyes darted between him and Laurel.

"If anyone knows anything, it would be better to hear about it before we get the principal involved," said Mr. Craven.

And with that, their happy moods were gone. Throughout the day, Calum and Laurel had fingers pointed at them and whispers said behind their backs. Calum overheard one girl say, "Laurel thinks she can do whatever she wants because her dad's a principal here."

"Must be nice," wheedled the other girl. "Wonder which one of her boyfriends helped—Calum or Hagen."

Laurel was still visibly upset at the lunch table.

"Ms. Itig keeps the key in plain sight," said Calum. "Anyone could have taken it during Night School."

Something tugged at Calum. Sure, anyone could have done it, but even with the key, it would have taken hours to unlock each lock and put them back on the locker. Calum doubted it would have been humanly possible for this prank to have been pulled during the short time the building had been opened for Night School.

Maybe it was the trickster? he thought.

For now, Laurel, still looked miserable. "Ignore Riley," said Calum. "By tomorrow they'll be talking about someone else."

Calum's prediction was not an accurate one. Several days had passed and many of the other sixth graders were still giving him and Laurel a hard time. One day in the hallway, they overheard Riley talking about "that spoiled principal's kid."

Laurel walked over to her and said, "I don't know how you did it, but I'll find out. Then you'll find out that sometimes it *is* handy to be the principal's kid."

"We'll see," said Riley.

The days crept by. February bumped right into March, and Hagen and Laurel were still at odds. Calum decided he'd better intervene or his two best friends would never reconcile. He thought he'd start with Laurel—maybe it was all a misunderstanding. He invited her to his house one night after dinner. He sat struggling with his words as he picked apart a slice of chocolate cake with his fork.

"You see, Laurel," he began, but Calum did not get to finish because he was suddenly no longer sitting in the Ranson's yellow kitchen.

Chapter Ten

The Grand Call

Calum stood in a circle below the thick, leafy branches of tall oaks surrounding the clearing. His mother was on his left, his grandfather beside her. It only took a second to realize where they were.

"Why are we in Aessea?" he asked.

"The Grand Call," said Kenzie.

"A death?" asked Calum. "Who?"

"Shh," hissed a voice to his right.

A tall figure moved away from the circle. Muscular and deeply tanned, he addressed the crowd, but looked straight at Uilleam. "As Keeper of the Aessea Mound, I have called you all to me. As a family, we celebrate the comings and goings of our clan. Please join hands."

The "shh-er" took Calum's right hand. Calum felt his mother grasp his left. As she took her father's hand, Kenzie looked very much like a child herself.

"Today we honor the life of Iris Lindsey," the Keeper announced.

Kenzie pulled Calum to her, breaking his hold on the Sidhe beside him.

Iris? thought Calum. One look at his grandfather and Calum knew this was no mistake.

"Oh, no," said Calum, his voice cracking.

"Iris left this world a short time ago. I was with her," said the Keeper. "She died peacefully, and with love in her heart. She will rest beside her beloved husband, Alistair. You have my deepest sympathies, Uilleam." He placed his hand on Uilleam's shoulder.

Kenzie sobbed into her father's chest. Calum watched tears roll down his grandfather's face. He hugged them both tightly, wanting to take away their sadness but feeling vastly inadequate in doing so. Kenzie regained her composure and called Tullia, who arrived instantly.

"I'm sorry for your loss," said Tullia.

"Please tell Salena I will be home tonight," said Uilleam.

"Calum and I will stay in Tusatha with Salena and Uilleam," said Kenzie. "Would you please bring Gus there?"

"I will," said Tullia, and then she disappeared. Not being a member of the Aessea clan, she was not permitted to be at their Grand Call.

Iris Lindsey's funeral was held three days later. As dictated by Sidhe tradition, it was a quiet gathering of immediate family members.

"My mother was a gentle soul who loved the earth," said Uilleam. "She taught me to find peace and comfort in the natural world. She was a great lady, and I will miss her." He placed several wildflowers on the top of her casket. "Be at peace, Mother. And may we find peace without you."

The air became heavy and settled on them like a thick dark

veil. Calum saw nothing past his own nose. His mouth had a metallic taste. The darkness lasted only seconds before it was slammed to the ground by cold air from above. When daylight returned, Iris' coffin had vanished. A sand-colored stone the size of a softball lay next to its mate, the marker of Alistair Lindsey's grave.

"I close the Grand Call and open the Aessea Mound," said Uilleam.

Salena and Gus arrived moments later. Salena took Uilleam's hand and Gus pulled Kenzie and Calum into his arms.

"I'm sorry about your mother, Uilleam," said Gus.

"Thank you, son." Uilleam looked down at Calum as they walked away from the grave markers. "You were only three years old the last time we were called to Aessea for a funeral. I'm sure you don't remember it."

"I don't," said Calum. "But I do remember that taste."

"What taste?" asked Gus.

"Iron," said Uilleam. "We taste it when we bury our dead."

"Why didn't they tell you and Kenzie about Iris first?" asked Calum. "It's mean to tell everyone at the same time."

"We're summoned here at the wishes of the dying person," said Uilleam. "They might call their family to them. But if they don't, the Keeper calls right after they pass. Iris probably didn't know it was her time."

"I want to show you something, Calum," said Kenzie. "This was Iris' charm bracelet. She left it to me because I was born on her birthday. There's a face for each child, grandchild, and great-grandchild. Here's yours," she said, lifting a silver face toward

Calum. "See? It has your birth date on it."

Calum flipped through the little faces. "It's too bad Hagen and Donnelly aren't here."

"You know they're not allowed to come to our Grand Call," said Kenzie.

"But it's not fair. She was Donnelly's grandma too," said Calum.

"Yes, but when Donnelly's mother married Torin, she broke ties with our clan and joined the Hobayeth," Uilleam explained.

"Did she have to?" asked Calum.

"No," said Uilleam. "My sister wanted to."

Calum and his family returned to Emerald Lake that evening. They were greeted in their own home by the Dunbar family, who had prepared a chicken casserole and fresh salad for supper. Calum didn't realize how hungry he was until he served himself a third helping.

"I'm sorry you couldn't come to the funeral, Donnelly. Are you all right?" asked Kenzie.

"Yeah," said Donnelly. "Even though I haven't seen Iris in a long time, I wish I could have been there."

"I'd like it if you would come with us when we go back to Aessea," said Uilleam. "I need to empty Iris' house. Mother was a collector. She had lots of dark Sidhe artifacts. I could use your help sorting it all out."

"I'd like that, Uilleam," said Donnelly. "Thanks."

There was a knock at the door and Gus rose from the table to answer. Laurel followed him back into the kitchen.

"Mom didn't want to bother you, but she asked me to bring this over." She set a cherry pie on the table.

"Thanks honey," said Kenzie. "It looks delicious. Please stay and have some with us."

"I can't. I need to get back." Laurel turned to Calum and Hagen. "But can I talk to you guys first?"

Calum nodded and led Laurel and Hagen into the game room. "I'm sorry about your great-grandmother," said Laurel as they sat down at the card table.

"Thanks," said Calum. Laurel seemed nervous, almost wary. Calum noticed she was avoiding his gaze. *Something's wrong.*

Hagen got up and slid the pocket door closed. *Of course there is, you disappeared right before her eyes.*

"There's something else," said Laurel. "I know what you are." Her eyes darted between Calum and Hagen.

Calum choked and coughed. "What we are?"

"I *know*," Laurel repeated, clutching her stone pendant.

"Okay," said Hagen. "What are we?"

"Sidhe," said Laurel. She stared into Hagen's eyes, waiting for him to contradict her. When he didn't, she continued. "I knew there was something different about you and your families, but I couldn't figure it out. It wasn't until you disappeared right in front of me that I put it together."

Calum sat in stunned silence. *She's not afraid.*

"How do you know about the Sidhe?" asked Hagen, still not admitting she was right.

"It was in the book Calum sold me," said Laurel.

"What's she talking about?" asked Hagen, his voice held a hint of accusation.

"A book she bought at Siopa Leabhar about faeries," Calum replied. "But that stuff's never right."

"Try me," said Laurel.

"Okay," said Hagen. "What's a polder?"

"Well, that depends on who's asking. For humans, a polder is a bit of land that used to be under water. For Sidhe, a polder is a bit of land that is surrounded by two circles. The outer circle makes the polder invisible to humans. The inner circle holds the thresholds."

"I need to get Donnelly," said Hagen, rising from the table. "Keep her here."

Calum knew how his uncle would react to Laurel knowing about them. "Don't Hagen," he said quickly. "Please don't tell Donnelly."

"That's what tipped me off at first," said Laurel. "You guys always calling your parents by their first name. You'd said it was an Irish tradition, but I know how that affects faeries. It strengthens the good ones, and weakens the bad ones. That's why the bad ones don't tell anyone their real name."

Calum stared at her in disbelief. After all the years of his wanting to share the secret, he never expected anyone to flat-out guess. "Most people would be freaking out right about now."

"I'm not like most people," said Laurel. "I've seen Sidhe magic before. I've had years to think about what I saw, study it. I'm not afraid."

Daniel, thought Calum.

We've got to do something. Hagen glared at Calum. *It isn't right she knows.*

No. She's our friend. Give her a chance.

"I think now would be a good time for you to explain about your brother," said Calum.

Laurel took a deep breath. "It was several years ago. Our parents took us camping at Fairy Stone Park in Virginia. I don't remember much about the trip, except for the day Daniel disappeared." Laurel glanced nervously at Hagen, who was now pacing the room. She recited a story she must have repeated to herself a thousand times.

"A song woke me and Daniel before sunrise. We listened for a few minutes and decided to follow it. I guess my parents didn't hear it, because Dad was snoring when we passed by their cabin room.

"Daniel grabbed a flashlight, and we walked into the woods behind our cabin. The woods got thicker, and it got darker the further we walked. I was scared and wanted to go back, but Daniel wanted to keep going. I stopped, refusing to go on, so angry with Daniel for not taking me back to the cabin. I yelled at him, but he ignored me and kept walking. I was watching him when he walked right into nothing. All that was left was his flashlight, lying inside a circle."

"What do you mean a circle?" asked Calum.

"One of *your* circles. A faerie circle," said Laurel. "The leaves and grass had been flattened, forming a perfect circle and Daniel's flashlight was in the middle."

Calum and Hagen exchanged worried looks.

Laurel continued her story without noticing their silent communication. "I started to go after the flashlight, but before I stepped into the circle I was pulled backwards. I turned around and saw a boy. I don't know where he came from, and I don't know how, but he was holding Daniel's flashlight. He handed it to me and turned me back toward the cabin. He also gave me this." Laurel held up the pendant that was forever hanging around her neck.

Hagen's eyes fixed on the Hobayeth mark. He moved away to put some distance between himself and the stone.

Laurel glared at him. "I know our moms think I'm madly in love with you, Hagen Dunbar," she said, her voice rising.

"Shh, keep it down or they'll hear you," Calum said in a warning tone.

"I don't care," Laurel said even louder.

"Everything all right in there?" called Gus.

"It's fine, Dad. Just joking around," said Calum.

"Keep your voice down, duine daonna," Hagen warned.

"Why don't you make me?"

"I just might."

"Hagen, don't." Calum had known Hagen all his life and knew when he was on the verge of losing control.

"I hate to disappoint you, Hagen," said Laurel, lowering her voice, "but the reason I stare at you is because you remind me of the boy who gave me this stone. When I'm around you, my memory becomes clearer. I can almost smell the scents and hear the sounds of that morning. I hope by strengthening my memory, I'll be able to find my brother." Laurel paused. Tears slid down her cheeks.

"Laurel, I'm sorry," said Calum. "We had no idea."

"No one does. You guys are the only ones I've ever told. Except for Mr. Girvan."

"Who's he?" asked Calum.

"A private investigator my parents hired to find Daniel," said Laurel. "He sends them a report every month." A full minute passed before she spoke again. "What did you call me, Hagen? *Duine daonna*? What does that mean?"

"It's Gaelic for human being," Hagen grumbled.

"He spends a lot of time in Ireland," said Calum. "Sometimes his Irish side comes out."

"You all seem so normal, so nice. I just don't understand it. How can you guys take someone's kid?" demanded Laurel.

"Our clans don't," Hagen said defensively.

"But other clans do," said Calum. "Well, did. It's against the law now."

"How do they do it?" asked Laurel.

"The circle you saw in the grass was made by Sidhe. It was a temporary threshold to their mound. If a human steps into the circle, they're trapped. We call these humans Additions because they're added to the clan."

"What's going to happen now?" asked Laurel.

"That depends on whether or not we can trust you to keep our secret," said Hagen.

"I'll keep your secret," said Laurel. She stared at Hagen, as if sizing him up. "For a price. I've searched for years for some explanation for Daniel's disappearance. Now that I've got it, if you help me find Daniel, I'll keep your secret."

"Sidhe don't take kindly to threats from duine daonna," said Hagen.

Calum saw the anger flash in Hagen's eyes. *Easy, cousin.*

"So think of it as a deal instead. Are you in or out?" asked Laurel, sliding her pendant across her necklace.

Calum stared at the Hobayeth mark. *We need her help. Maybe that's what happened to Finley.*

Maybe, thought Hagen. "I don't like it, but I'm in." He turned to Laurel. "But we're in charge, and you'll have to do what we say."

Laurel looked at him, puzzled. "What can I do? I'm not faerie."

"No, but your stone belongs to one," said Hagen. "The small symbol is the mark of the Hobayeth. I'm guessing the other mark belongs to the Fairy Stone."

"Your stone might be a token, a key into their mound," said Calum.

"So take it." Laurel reached to unfasten the chain.

"We can't take it," Hagen said impatiently. "In order for a token to work properly, it can only be given away by a clan member. You're not a Fairy Stone Sidhe. If you give the token away, it will lose its magic. If I take the token from you, it will disintegrate in my hand. That's how the token is protected. And even if I had a token of my own, I still wouldn't be able to rescue Daniel."

"Why not?" Calum raised an eyebrow.

"Additions can only be claimed by a blood relative. So, we need your help, Laurel. Are *you* in or out?" Hagen asked abruptly.

Laurel smiled a sad smile. "It's been so long. After all these years. Sometimes I've been afraid I'd imagined the whole thing." She wiped her eyes. "I mean, I never saw any proof your world existed, other than what I thought had happened to Daniel."

"I'll bet you have seen proof." Hagen's tone softened. "Have you ever seen a bubble moving across a field that seemed to come from nowhere?"

Laurel thought for a second. "Yes. I really have."

"A stray bubble is a piece of the Sidhe world that has spilled out. If you followed the bubble, you'd see it travels forever without bursting."

Laurel looked skeptical. "I'm sitting here listening to you, and at the same time it sounds crazy. Like it can't be real, you know?"

"It is real. And I can prove you have experience with our magic," said Calum. He strode to the fireplace, retrieving the vase of Particulars. He pulled the honey-colored twig from the vase. "Do you remember what Kenzie said when you handed this to her?

"Secrets," said Laurel. "I'd tell one and learn one."

"After a prediction comes true, it appears at the bottom of the Particular with the name of the person the prediction was made for. Look here," said Calum. "It says, *Secrets. Laurel.*"

Laurel took the Particular from Calum and studied the words. "I told one and I learned one." She turned the Particular over and over in her hands. "What's all this at the top?" she asked. "It looks like squished up words."

"The Particular records every prediction it makes," said Hagen. "Over time, the older predictions move to the tip. Here, I'll show you." He took the Particular from her. "*Defluo.*" Hagen tapped the bottom of the Particular on the ground. The letters at the tip spread out and flowed down, making the words at the bottom now impossible to read.

Calum saw Laurel's name carved in the middle of the Particular and leaned in to get a better look. Before he could read the words, they formed a pile of scribbles at the bottom.

"So, are you in?" asked Hagen, more gently this time.

"In," said Laurel. "Definitely in."

"Me too," said Calum.

"Just what I need." Hagen sighed. "A duine daonna and an untrained Sidhe stomping through the Otherworld looking for an Addition."

"But you *will* do it?" Laurel asked desperately.

"Yeah," said Hagen. "We'll do it."

"You'll do what?" Donnelly suddenly appeared in the doorway.

Calum jumped at his uncle's voice. "We'll—"

"Save it, Calum," said Hagen. "They already know. You know they do."

Calum paused momentarily, calling his grandfather to him.

"Uilleam is already here," said Donnelly. "Kenzie called him. He's waiting for you and Laurel in the leabharlann. Hagen, you come with me. We're to get the bittersweets."

"The what?" asked Laurel.

"Too many questions, duine daonna," said Donnelly. "You

already know more than you should."

Calum cast a glance at Hagen. *Donnelly wouldn't…he couldn't take Laurel's memory away. I won't let him.*

"Anything you want to ask me, Calum?" asked Donnelly, raising one eyebrow.

Calum shook his head, but he couldn't shake his worries. Too late, he realized he hadn't protected his thoughts and his uncle must have read them.

"I think you'd better work on shutting that door," said Donnelly. He walked out with Hagen, leaving Calum and Laurel in the game room.

CHAPTER ELEVEN
THE FAIRY STONE

Calum led Laurel to the library, where he pointed to one of the ceramic tiles in the floor "The leabharlann's down there."

"You're kidding. We're going through that?" asked Laurel.

"It's easy, watch." Calum moved his hands in a sweeping motion. "*Amplifico*."

Nothing happened. Calum blushed deeply. He was so anxious to get Laurel away from Donnelly, he couldn't focus. *Got to get a grip on my nerves.* He sucked in a deep breath and tried two more times before the tile stretched wider and taller, rising on its edge perpendicular to the floor. Calum and Laurel entered the passageway and walked down a winding staircase. Knowing Uilleam waited for them at the bottom of the stairs, Calum began to relax. "That's the most interesting part of this room," he said. "Everything else down here's a snore fest."

An earthy smell filled Calum's nostrils. Blackened sconces lined stone walls in a downward spiral, each with a tiny black candle that automatically lighted as they approached. They reached the leabharlann and followed a curved path between piles of books and unlabeled boxes to where Uilleam's tall frame was bent over a heavy writing desk. Working by candlelight, his red hair shone like copper as he reviewed an aged catalog of clan artifacts.

"Uilleam," said Calum, relieved to see his grandfather's face. "You're going to help, right?" he asked, anxiously.

"*Windesco*," said Uilleam. "Before I can answer that, I need to know what's going on." He smiled and offered his right hand to Laurel. "I am Uilleam."

Laurel looked at Calum and mouthed, "Windesco?"

"He always says that," whispered Calum. "I don't know why."

"It's nice to meet you Uilleam." Laurel shook his hand.

"Please, sit down and tell me your words," said Uilleam. Laurel sat on a leather ottoman and told him about Daniel. When she held up the pendant, Uilleam's gaze locked onto it. "May I see that please?"

Laurel raised the pendant toward Uilleam.

"Hagen was right," he said. "These are the marks of the Hobayeth and the Fairy Stone clans."

"The park rangers said these stones were easy to find," said Laurel.

"Some fairy stones are. But not ones like this," said Uilleam. "I think I need to tell you about the Fairy Stone before we go on. They were a gentle clan, peace loving, nature loving. Years ago, the duine daonna petitioned the State of Virginia to develop several hundred acres of Fairy Stone Park. The faeries that lived in those woods scattered fairy stones by the thousands, hoping to convince the State of Virginia the park was a special and historical area that shouldn't be disturbed. They succeeded. In fact, it's one of the few times faeries have been able to halt the thinning of our world.

Remind me to tell you about Stonehenge another time." He smiled at her. "Your stone is similar to one of the fairy stones, but it's actually a token used by that clan to enter their mound."

"So their threshold's sealed?" asked Laurel.

"You *have* been doing your homework," said Uilleam. "Yes, it's sealed. And you need their token to get in or out. I'm certain Daniel has been what the duine daonna call 'pixie led'. That means he was tricked and added to their clan. You were given the token by someone whom we must assume is a part of that clan. The token is your invitation to visit their mound."

"That's weird," said Calum. "If a Sidhe betrayed his own clan like that, he'd get banished. Why would anyone do that?"

"Why indeed?" asked Uilleam. "As you can think of no reason to betray your clan to a stranger, a strange duine daonna at that—no offense, Laurel—what does it mean?"

"That whoever gave Laurel the token was not a member of the Fairy Stone clan," said Calum. "But then, how would he have a token to give away?"

"That's a good question," said Uilleam. "Another good question is why Laurel remembers anything at all? Why didn't he clear her memory?"

"Sidhe can do that?" asked Laurel.

"We can and do," said Uilleam. "Quite often."

Calum shivered, thinking of Donnelly waiting for them upstairs. "That Sidhe let Laurel keep her memory, and gave her the token because he wanted her to find Daniel."

"If Daniel's in Fairy Stone, and I've been invited there, I want to go. Now." Laurel jumped to her feet. "Please Calum, take me to their town."

"Sit down, child," Uilleam said gently.

Laurel stood firm, her arms folded across her chest.

Calum stared at her. *She's pretty brave for a duine daonna.*

"When moral courage feels that it is in the right, there is no personal daring for which it is incapable. Leigh Hunt was a great duine daonna poet," said Uilleam. He smiled at Laurel, but she didn't budge. "I agree you must go to their mound to seek your brother. But there's more for us to understand, and obviously much more for you to learn before you may go. Town, indeed." He chuckled. "We live in mounds. Please, sit down." This time Laurel obeyed. "I will go to Fairy Stone Park tonight and look for a threshold to the Fairy Stone Mound."

"What can I do?" asked Laurel.

"More important is what you can't do," said Uilleam. "You can't tell anyone about what you've learned. For one thing, who would believe you? And there's no sense in concerning your parents. They've already lost one child. They don't need to worry about losing you."

"I'll do whatever you say, I just want Daniel home."

"I believe you," said Uilleam.

Calum relaxed. He knew Uilleam would protect her from Donnelly's desire to erase her memory.

"Tell me, Laurel, when did Daniel disappear?" asked Uilleam.

"Almost seven years ago, during Memorial Day weekend," said Laurel. "May twenty-seventh."

"Time is hurrying us," said Uilleam. "We must retrieve Daniel before midnight on May twenty-seventh."

"Why before then?" asked Laurel.

"If an Addition isn't rescued within seven years, he's stuck in the Otherworld forever," said Uilleam. "Daniel will never leave because he'll be convinced he never wants to." He lifted his candle. "Let's get back to the others. We need to get started."

Calum and Laurel followed him upstairs and to the kitchen where everyone else waited.

"Do you have the bittersweet berries?" asked Uilleam.

"Right here," said Hagen, indicating a wooden bowl on the table. It was filled with orange berries, their golden husks hanging loosely at the tops.

"Our secret is safe with Laurel," Uilleam said to Donnelly.

Donnelly didn't speak but nodded his agreement.

"I shouldn't be long," said Uilleam.

"I'll go with you," said Donnelly. "This has something to do with the Hobayeth. You'll need my help."

"You're right. I do," said Uilleam. "I need your help here."

Donnelly rose from the table. "You don't understand, Uilleam. The Hobayeth are dangerous."

Uilleam's eyes narrowed. "I understand better than you think. Which is why I want you to stay where you will be of more use. And don't worry about me." He raised an eyebrow. "I know how to handle the Hobayeth."

Donnelly let out a sigh, raising both palms in the air. "Fine. Have it your way, but we'll be watching. If I see anything, I'm coming right away."

"Me too," said Kenzie.

"We all will," said Tullia.

"Agreed. It will be one big party," said Uilleam. "But it won't be necessary." He turned and disappeared.

Laurel gave a soft squeak.

"He just went through the threshold," Calum explained. "Like what's in the polder." He led Laurel to the table, where she sat down timidly.

Kenzie gave Laurel a kind smile before pushing the bowl of bittersweet berries to the middle of the table. She put her hands on the wooden bowl, turning it halfway around left, right, and left again. When she let go, the berries spun furiously in a counter-clockwise direction in the motionless bowl. An image of Uilleam rose inside the spinning berries. He stood at the entrance to Fairy Stone Park. Calum watched the scene play out before him as if he were watching a 3D movie. Two park rangers worked to secure the gate, seemingly unaware of him.

Uilleam strolled down a man-made path deep into the woods. The path turned left and looped back to the park. He veered off the path and headed toward the right side of a large boulder. He ambled through the woods, stopping here and there to study the way the leaves moved in the light breeze or the direction in which branches were shaped on an old oak tree. He chuckled as the toe of his shoe nudged a rusty watering can.

"That's their post," said Hagen.

Calum looked at him curiously.

"Something ordinary out of the ordinary," Hagen explained. "It points to their threshold."

At that moment, Calum caught his breath when he saw a

greasy blob of a man creep up behind Uilleam. The man's rust-colored skin was covered in scars. Barbed wire held his hair in a long stringy ponytail. His shirt was loose, but his pants appeared tattooed to his skin. Both were covered in slime and filth.

Uilleam did not turn around. "Say your words."

"I say *my* words?" replied the man, indignation in his tone. "You're the one who should state your purpose, wandering around where you don't belong."

Uilleam gathered himself to his full height and turned to face the man. "I am Uilleam Lindsey, and I belong wherever I wish to be."

This seemed to change the situation, for the other voice now spoke in a false friendly tone. "No harm meant, Uilleam. Please, call me Brownshire." He offered his right hand, but Uilleam ignored it.

"Why would I call you that?" asked Uilleam. "It's clearly not your name. But I will learn your true name before we meet again."

Brownshire glared at Uilleam. "I am the Keeper of the Fairy Stone Mound. We sensed your presence. What do you seek?"

"You are the Keeper? Forgive me, but that does not seem correct. My guess is you've stolen this role rather than earned it by birthright. Keeper is not usually given to someone who is only part Sidhe." He looked the squat man up and down. "Where is the true Keeper?"

Brownshire once again found his courage. "I'm the Keeper, like it or not. State your purpose or you will have to leave."

"You may leave if you wish," Uilleam responded. "But I will leave only when I'm ready to do so." He turned his back on the stubby man.

Brownshire disappeared with a loud thunderclap.

Uilleam continued searching the wood unbothered. A short time later he said, "I think that's enough for now, daughter. I'll see you soon." He made a wide gesture with his hands and closed his fingers one at a time. The bittersweet berries fell back into the bowl and Calum and the others were left in silence.

Twenty minutes later, Uilleam returned to the kitchen. Calum felt the tension leave his body when he realized his grandfather was safe.

"It's about time. We were getting worried," said Kenzie, rising from the table.

"There was no need, for as you can see I'm fine." His green eyes met hers. "I found these." He fished around his coat pocket and he handed Donnelly several stones. "They're like the one Laurel has, but without the Hobayeth mark. I didn't find tokens, nor did I expect to. No Sidhe would carelessly throw about their token."

"Did you see any Fairy Stone Sidhe?" asked Calum.

"No," said Uilleam. "I believe they've abandoned their mound, and I think the Hobayeth are responsible."

"I don't understand why the Hobayeth would mark another clan's token," said Hagen. "Or why they would have driven the Fairy Stone out of their mound."

"The Hobayeth wouldn't, but *a* Hobayeth might," said Donnelly.

"Torin," said Tullia, grinding her teeth. "So that's where he went."

"Yes, but that is not where he is now," said Uilleam. "I'm certain the Fairy Stone Mound is empty. It's ironic the Fairy Stone won one of the few battles against the duine daonna only to be driven out of their mound by other Sidhe."

"Now that we know where Torin is, I'd like to ask him what he knows about Finley's disappearance," said Tullia.

"You can't ask Torin yet," said Uilleam. "We really don't know where he is. We only know where he was last."

"And when the time comes, I'll do the asking," said Donnelly.

"Who is this Torin?" Laurel whispered to Calum.

"I'll tell you who he is." Donnelly backed his chair away from the table. "Torin Garvey Dunbar is the Keeper of the Hobayeth clan. He's also my father."

Laurel's hand flew to her necklace, and she clutched it tightly. Donnelly continued, "Torin was obsessed with power. When I was a kid, I realized he would stop at nothing to get what he wanted. I remember one time watching him whip a member of our clan because he didn't provide an Addition to work in our fields. I begged my father to stop beating the man. I told him I would work in the man's place. Torin said I would be the next Keeper of the Hobayeth and he would never permit me to work as a servant. That evening, my mother let me know I had disappointed her as well. I couldn't believe my parents were so cruel. I fantasized that I had become a member of my clan by mistake. My sister, Bari, agreed with my parents, but my younger sister, Alana, wasn't sure which side to choose. It was for her sake I stayed with the Hobayeth for several more years. But when I met Tullia, I decided to move away from my clan and move on with my life."

"Torin created quite a stir when he protested the Additions Ban," said Tullia. "His only support came through intimidation. Thankfully the Ban passed, but many Sidhe were still afraid of him."

"We wanted to question Torin about Finley," said Uilleam. "But someone warned him and he disappeared. In order to keep peace between the clans, the Hobayeth banished Torin."

"And although I no longer associated with him, it wasn't long before other Sidhe made the connection between me and my father," said Donnelly. "Tullia and I thought it best if we left the Otherworld and we moved here. When I turned my back on the Hobayeth, they banished me."

"How awful," said Laurel.

"I think," said Donnelly, casting a glance at Hagen, "it would have been far worse for me to remain with my clan."

Tullia rubbed small circles on Donnelly's back.

"But that Hobayeth mark on your Fairy Stone makes me think they never really banished Torin. You have a valuable token Laurel," said Uilleam.

"Why?" asked Laurel.

"Your token may get you into the Fairy Stone *and* Hobayeth Mounds," said Hagen.

"If we ever find them," Calum blurted.

"That's enough talk for now," said Kenzie. "I told Andrea I'd bring Laurel home after supper. And Dad, you haven't even eaten yet. You must be hungry."

"No thanks, MecKenzie," said Uilleam. "I need to get home to my bride. I've never been away from her for more than twenty-four hours, and today will be no different." He turned to Laurel. "I'll speak to Connor tomorrow to see if he has any ideas about Daniel. Just don't get your hopes up." He cupped her chin in his hand. "I'm afraid if Torin's got Daniel—Well there's not much hope we'll find him. I'm sorry, Laurel." He released her and turned to leave. "I'll be in touch if I learn anything new." He crossed the threshold without another word.

CHAPTER TWELVE

DONNELLY

The weeks passed with no word from Uilleam about Daniel, Finley, or Torin. Calum noticed Laurel had become more and more anxious as Memorial Day drew nearer. They were running out of time. The Friday before spring break, Calum invited Hagen and Laurel to an all-night video gaming session at his house, hoping to relieve some of her anxiety.

They had completed three levels of Hero's Revenge before the doorbell announced their pizza delivery. It was such a beautiful night they decided to eat their supper on the back deck. Gus started a small fire in the brick pit, and Kenzie brought out marshmallows, chocolate bars, and graham crackers for Calum and his friends to make s'mores for dessert. Calum cleared his throat. Taking the hint, the adults returned to the kitchen, leaving Calum and his friends alone with a large pizza and several bottles of iced soda.

Calum's mouth watered as soon as he smelled the pineapple covered pie. He had devoured his third slice when Laurel spoke.

"I forgot to tell you what happened right after school today. I was in the girls' room when Susie came in crying. Kirby was with her."

Calum hoped it wasn't anything serious. He liked Susie. "Was it Riley?"

Laurel shook her head. "No. Susie told Kirby that her dad lost his job."

"That's not good," said Calum. He wondered how they would manage with Susie's dad out of work. He pushed the pizza box away, his appetite gone. "Did she say how?"

"She said her dad went fishing a few weeks ago," said Laurel. "He ran into a stranger at the lake. Since then he's been saying *they* are going to get him. Susie said he goes out every night looking for them. He lost his job because he kept falling asleep at work."

Hagen shook his head. "I should have said something."

"About what?" asked Calum.

"The calling. Only I wasn't sure. I mean, I didn't really know what it was."

"What are you talking about?" asked Laurel.

"The Hobayeth call," said Hagen. "I heard it a few weeks ago. It wasn't like the call I hear when my mom or someone in Tusatha wants me. This call was more like a question, asking if any Hobayeth were in the area."

"And you didn't think to mention this?" asked Calum.

Hagen nodded at Laurel. "How could I, without tipping off Donnelly?"

Calum knew what he was thinking. "So now what do we do?"

"I'll check it out," said Hagen. "It's got to have something to do with Susie's dad."

"You can't be serious," said Laurel. "It's too dangerous. You need to tell Donnelly."

"He can't, Laurel," said Calum. "The first thing Donnelly would do is…well, he'd think you were involved because no one knows why you were given that Hobayeth stone. He'd erase your memory."

"It's my memory, my choice. Right?" Laurel said defiantly. "I say you tell Donnelly."

"I'm not going to do that," said Hagen. "Uilleam doesn't think the Hobayeth or the Fairy Stone are here, remember? And no one even answered the call. I'm not going to tell Donnelly because if I do, you'll be of no use to us. There's more than Daniel at risk here. You see it, don't you Calum?"

Calum did. Daniel's unsolved disappearance was too close to home. This might be what they were waiting for, a clue to bring them closer to Finley. If they didn't take this chance, they might not get another one. "I think we should both go," said Calum. "We can do it tonight if Laurel covers for us. Will you?"

"No," Laurel said flatly.

"If you're not gonna help, you should just go home." Hagen was getting angry.

"I'm not going to cover for you, because I'm coming with you. We made a deal, remember?"

"Okay." Calum raised his hand to stop the argument before it started. "You can come too. We'll leave tonight after Kenzie and Gus go to bed."

They stayed up late, roasting marshmallows and eating

s'mores until the fire burned out. Calum poured water into the pit, and they quietly stepped inside the kitchen. He tiptoed upstairs to see if his parents were asleep. When he heard Gus snoring, he knew it was safe to go. As they crept through the kitchen to the back door, Wrecks began whining.

"You can't come with us, boy." Calum grabbed a rawhide chew from a bag on the floor of the pantry. "This will keep you busy." Wrecks took the treat and trotted to the game room.

Calum, Hagen, and Laurel eased out of the house and into the pitch black of midnight.

"Tell me how it happened," said Laurel. "With Finley."

"We were playing outside at Hagen's house in Tusatha," said Calum. "Mud splashed into my eyes and I couldn't see."

"I took him inside to get help," said Hagen. "When we went back out, Finley was gone."

"And you guys think Torin took him?"

"We never got to ask, because Torin disappeared that night," said Hagen. "I can't believe I'm related to *him*." He stopped walking.

"What's wrong?" asked Calum.

"I've heard the Hobayeth call before. The day Finley was taken," said Hagen, despair in his voice. "I should have told someone."

"It wasn't your fault, Hagen," said Calum. "You were only five. You had no idea what you heard, plus you were trying to help me." He put his arm on Hagen's shoulder. "I say we find this Hobayeth and make him tell us where the clan is. Then whoever is responsible will pay for what they've done."

145

"Even if it is my grandfather," Hagen said bitterly.

"Let's keep going," said Calum, taking the lead. They continued walking until they reached a clearing in the middle of the woods.

"Are we going through?" Laurel asked nervously. "I mean, through the polder?"

"No, this is a shortcut to Devil's Peak," said Calum. "Susie's house is just on the other side of the reserve."

When they arrived at the edge of the Turnbill property, they hid behind a wooden tool shed and sat down on a thick layer of pine needles. Hagen pointed to where Mr. Turnbill sat, his back propped against a young pine tree.

Calum heard laughter, evil laughter coming from the other side of the backyard.

Bob Turnbill staggered to the middle of the yard, swinging a crowbar. "Come here you cowards. Come and get yours!" he shouted to no one.

"I don't see anything, do you?" asked Laurel.

"No, but I hear it. The Hobayeth calling," said Hagen. He stood, listening to a sound only he could hear.

Laurel grabbed his hand and yanked him backwards. "What are you doing? Sit down," she hissed.

"Who's that man over there?" Calum glanced back at Hagen and Laurel. She still clutched Hagen's hand.

In that instant, a rock struck Mr. Turnbill on his leg, which led him to more fits of yelling and swinging. A gust of wind blew from the pines, causing Mr. Turnbill's shirt to flap in the breeze, exposing some type of weapon. A tall man ran from the tree line toward Mr. Turnbill. Even in the darkness, Calum recognized him.

"I agree with Bob, it's rather cowardly of you to torment him when you're invisible, Kegan," Donnelly said in a voice that was not his own. He grabbed a handful of nothing. A man with coal black hair instantly materialized. Donnelly held him by the throat. The man moaned in pain, struggling to break free.

"Donnelly, what are you doing here?" asked Mr. Turnbill. "Who is this man?"

"It doesn't matter, Bob," soothed Donnelly in an eerily calm voice. "Hagen, Calum," he called. "A little help?"

Calum swallowed hard, knowing they were busted.

"Just you two," Donnelly added.

Hagen darted from behind the shed to his father's side. Calum rose and followed him.

"Catch Bob." Donnelly laid his free hand on the man's shoulder. Bob's eyes glazed over and he collapsed. Calum and Hagen caught him in time to break his fall, easing him to the ground.

Still struggling against Donnelly, Kegan's arms flung wildly. Donnelly lifted him several inches into the air and shook him violently. "Now, dear brother, you will leave and never return. Do you understand? Try to guess why. Take your time, I have all night."

Calum had never heard anyone speak this way, and the tone of his uncle's voice gave him a shiver. It seemed Donnelly enjoyed terrorizing the Sidhe.

Kegan, twitching in pain, mumbled an incoherent response.

Donnelly gave him a twisted smile. "Good for you, you got it right. You'll leave him alone because I'll find out if you don't. You only imagine this to be painful," Donnelly snarled as Kegan screamed in agony. "If we ever meet again, you'll know what real pain is." Donnelly lifted his hand and Kegan disappeared in a blaze of red flames.

Calum jumped, tripping over Mr. Turnbill's form on the ground.

"You okay?" asked Donnelly.

"Yeah," said Calum, embarrassed.

"Let's get Bob back to his house," said Donnelly. They half carried, half dragged the unconscious man up the porch steps. Calum grunted as they laid Bob on a creaking swing. "Rest and forget," Donnelly whispered, gently touching Bob's arm who seemed to drift into a deeper sleep.

"How did you know we were here?" asked Hagen.

"You're not the only one who heard the call," said Donnelly. "It was strange, after all these years."

"Who was that?" asked Calum as they walked back toward the trees where Laurel waited.

"One of the Hobayeth," said Donnelly. "I remember him from my childhood. He's a nomad now, just roaming, looking for his clan. Don't worry, he won't be back."

"How can you be sure?" asked Laurel.

"He knows who I am, and knows my threats are…more like promises."

Calum looked at Laurel. He hoped Donnelly wasn't talking about her.

"Look, I know why you came here, Hagen. You heard the

calling. I get it. You're old enough to go into the mounds, and I won't be able to stop you from going to any mound you want, but you've got to be careful around the Hobayeth. Understand?"

"Yeah," said Hagen. "Sorry, Donnelly."

"As for you, Calum, Kenzie is going to have forty fits over this."

Calum imagined the trouble he'd find at home.

"Don't sweat it. I'll cover for you. This time," said Donnelly. "There's really no reason for Kenzie to know you were here."

"Thanks," said Calum, breathing a little easier.

As they continued walking, they were soon surrounded by the thick trees of the reserve. Calum thought about what Donnelly had said. *He's wrong. Kegan will keep looking until he finds the mound. It's got to be close, or he wouldn't be here.*

Calum cringed, certain Donnelly had read his thoughts, but his uncle didn't seem to notice.

Donnelly escorted them right to Calum's front porch. "I think it would be best if you all stay in the rest of the night." Calum nodded and thanked his uncle again. Hagen gave Donnelly a hug.

"See you tomorrow," said Donnelly.

As soon as Calum bolted the front door, Laurel pulled him and Hagen into the game room. She closed the door behind them. "I know Kegan."

"How?" Hagen asked doubtfully.

"He's Mr. Girvan," said Laurel. "The private detective my parents hired to find Daniel. If he's a Hobayeth, I'll bet he knows where Daniel is."

"We're already ahead of you," said Calum.

"Then let's go find him!"

Calum and Hagen didn't move.

"What are you waiting for?" Laurel demanded.

"Donnelly is outside, waiting to see if we'll go out again," Hagen said. "If we do, he'll definitely tell Kenzie what's going on."

"So what do we do?" she asked, visibly frustrated.

"We wait until morning," said Calum. "Let Donnelly think we believe Kegan's a nomad. When things calm down, we'll go."

Calum's parents left early the next morning to take inventory at the bookstore in preparation of the upcoming tourist season. Calum and Hagen sat in the guest room as Laurel packed her overnight bag. Buster wound his body between Calum's ankles, trying to get his attention. The cat soon lost his patience and slunk out of the room.

"The Fairy Stone Mound has to be in Devil's Peak," said Calum. "Think about it. The Fairy Stone were forced from their home in a state park. They'd be drawn to a reserve, and Devil's Peak backs up to the Turnbill property. I'll bet you anything it's there."

"Only one way to find out," said Hagen.

"Well, I'm ready." Laurel paused, twisting a section of her long blonde hair around her fingers. "But I wouldn't be able to forgive myself if something happened to you guys."

"We'll be fine," said Calum. "We'll only be there an hour. After that, we'll leave because of the new law."

"But if Daniel is there, how will we get him out?" asked Laurel.

150

"Your token. It gets you and one other person into and out of their mound," said Calum. "You can bring me in, and then take Daniel out. I'll leave anyway because of the law."

"I should be the one to go with her," said Hagen. "I know more about them than you do."

"They know you're the grandson of the Queen. You'd be safer and more useful if you stayed behind," said Calum.

"Gee, thanks *Uilleam*," said Hagen, irritated. "How do you figure?"

"You can be our messenger. If we have problems, you'll have to call Donnelly. You're the only one who can."

"I thought you guys shared your call?" asked Laurel.

"The Aessea and Tusatha do," said Calum. "But Donnelly's Hobayeth. Only Hagen can call him."

Hagen looked disappointed, but nodded. "Okay. But I don't like it. And you guys have to stick together. It may sound like no big deal walking into their mound, with the new law and all, but it's risky for a duine daonna to visit a dark clan under any circumstances."

"But if we stay together, we'll be all right?" asked Laurel.

Calum heard the worry behind her question. "Yes, as long as you stay with me." He removed the ring from his finger. "This will bind us together. If you lose your token, and by that, I mean if one of them reclaims it, I can take you out of the mound." *But I can only take one of them. There has to be another way.*

"A glove," said Hagen.

"It's really annoying when you guys do that," said Laurel.

"Sorry. There's an old story about duine daonna sneaking into a mound," Calum explained. "If the duine daonna leaves a glove in the circle, they can use that as a token to get out."

"It might work," said Hagen. "But no one knows for sure because no one's tried it with a dark clan. You could be trapped."

"I don't care about the risks," said Laurel. "I'll go, because if I don't I'll be trapped forever in a different way. I'll go to this mound. If it doesn't work then I'll go to another, and another, until I find him."

Hagen smiled in approval.

"So, when do we go?" asked Laurel.

"Tonight at seven," said Calum. "While everyone else is in Aessea at Iris' house."

"Don't you have to go with them?" asked Laurel.

"No. I told Kenzie I wasn't comfortable going through Iris' things."

"And Tullia's staying home with Brytes and Will," said Hagen.

"But, can you get back here tonight, Laurel?" asked Calum.

"Yeah. I'll tell my parents we're still playing video games. I'm sure they'll let me stay over again." Laurel picked up her bag. She looked uncertain about their plan.

Calum smiled at her. "Don't worry. We'll keep you safe. I promise."

"I know you will," she said, shaking the worry from her expression. "I'll see you at seven." She turned and carried her bag through the door.

She's pretty brave, thought Calum.

152

Let's hope she's brave enough, Hagen replied.

Calum and Hagen stayed close to the house that day. When Kenzie and Gus returned home, the boys acted as if they were worn out from staying up all night. After supper, they lounged on the sofas in the family room. Calum flipped disinterestedly through channels on the television.

Donnelly arrived at seven. He checked on the boys, and satisfied they were too exhausted to move, he, Kenzie, and Gus quietly slipped through the threshold on their way to Aessea Mound. Laurel arrived ten minutes later, carrying a leather glove.

"Will this work?" she asked.

"We'll see. But remember, it's just a back-up," said Calum, smiling encouragingly.

At sunset, they walked together to Devil's Peak Reserve.

"The trees are thick," said Calum, looking around the forest. "They'll send a message easily."

"Look," said Hagen, "I still think I should go with you."

"We've been over this. If you come with us, there will be no one here to get a message to Donnelly if we need help," said Calum.

"I know, I know," said Hagen. "I just wish I could do more."

"What was that?" Laurel grabbed Hagen's arm.

"What was what?" asked Calum.

"I thought I saw someone over there watching us." She pointed to a cluster of white azaleas.

"I don't see anyone," said Hagen. "Don't let your imagination run away with you."

"Don't worry," Laurel snapped. She immediately flushed with embarrassment and stammered an apology.

"Hey, maybe you did see someone," said Hagen. "This is a popular place. Lots of people hike the trail." He pulled a stone from his pocket and passed it to Calum. "The kyanite from Rebeccah."

Calum put the kyanite in his own pocket. "We'd better get going," he said, taking a deep breath. "I'll send a message as soon as we get through their threshold. Wait here for us."

Hagen clapped him on the back. "I will. I'll be right here."

"We're counting on it," said Calum.

Chapter Thirteen

Devil's Peak

Calum and Laurel encountered several people on the hiking trail, all on their way out of Devil's Peak Reserve. Most hikers were friendly, but one girl positively glared at Calum as she passed by. She had black eyes, glossy black hair, and a dark complexion. Although she smiled at them, hers was an unkind smile, more like a scowl.

"Who's she?" asked Laurel as they passed the girl.

"No idea. Must be a tourist." Calum pointed through the woods. "There's the end of the trail."

"How will we find their mound?"

"Their post. We'll know it when we see it," said Calum. "It'll be something that looks out of place."

It had been at least twenty minutes since they had passed the unpleasant girl when Calum said, "Look there. It's a watering can. Just like before, when Uilleam was looking for them. Remember? It's at a right angle to the first pine tree we've come across. It's pointing to the left."

They wandered through the woods for another ten minutes without finding the mound.

"I think we messed up," said Calum. "Maybe we've gone the wrong way."

They turned around to retrace their steps when Calum heard a "meow."

"Whisper?" said Laurel. "What are you doing out here?" Whisper, being a fairly decent cat, didn't answer, but merely looked up at Laurel with his amber colored eyes and purred. He nuzzled her leg and headed in the direction they had been traveling. Laurel looked at Calum, who gave a shrug and the two followed Whisper deeper into the woods.

"There's a clearing," said Calum. "It's got to be in there."

"Thanks, Whisper," said Laurel, scratching the black-and-white cat behind his ears. "Now, please go home."

Whisper gave another meow, turned around, and scurried back to the trail. Calum watched the cat and realized he only appeared to be heading home. He carefully and quietly crept behind two gray boulders, continuing to follow Calum and Laurel with his eyes. *Just like a cat*, thought Calum. *Doing whatever they like.*

"There it is," said Calum, pointing to a circular path on the ground. They stopped just at the edge of the circle. "Are you ready?"

Laurel peered into the middle of the circle but didn't answer.

"If you've changed your mind, we can find another way," said Calum.

"No. It's just…this looks exactly like the circle from my memory."

"I think it would be a good idea if we hold hands. You know, while we're in their mound?" He held his hand out to Laurel and she took it in her own. Calum's hand was clammy, but he couldn't tell if it was his hand or Laurel's that was doing the sweating.

They took one step. Laurel dropped her glove inside the circle before her foot touched down.

Calum heard a hiss. *Whisper?* He looked for the cat, but only saw the strange girl from the hiking trail. She stared at him with a wicked grin on her face. Calum thought he saw Hagen intercept her, but he lost track of them when he and Laurel passed into Devil's Peak Mound.

Calum looked around, trying to orient himself. He pulled Laurel behind a weathered shed. "I have to mark the place we came in." He took the kyanite crystal out of his backpack and tied it to the picket of an old wooden gate. "This is your temporary threshold. If we get separated, come back here and get back to the circle. Okay? Laurel?"

She stared trance-like into space. Her face was pale, her hair stuck to her neck like wet grass.

"Here, drink this," said Calum. His hands shook as he pulled a tiny epidote bottle from a cord around his neck. He held the bottle to Laurel's lips and poured clear liquid into her mouth. "Do you feel better?"

"A little," Laurel said weakly. "Where'd you get that?"

"I made it. It's one of the verses carved in the stacks at Siopa Leabhar."

"I just felt so weird." Laurel shook her head. "Like something bad was about to happen. It was like that day of the tornado."

"That's because we're surrounded by dark Sidhe."

Laurel's eyes darted from the shed to the trees.

"You've got to trust me," Calum said, squeezing her hand.

"I do." Laurel squeezed back.

"We don't have much time before one of the Fairy Stone comes to meet us. I have to send a message to Hagen so he knows we got in. Are you okay now?"

Laurel nodded.

"Sit here for a second, I'll be right back." Calum jogged a few yards to a stand of strangler figs, turning back every few paces to keep an eye on Laurel.

Devil's Peak Mound was different from any of the other mounds Calum had visited. There was a sulfur-like stench he recognized from learning dark magic. Tiny purple morning glories battled the air to show their colors. The flowers only lasted a second before snapping, and disappearing in puffs of smoke as if no beauty was allowed in this place. The other colors in this mound were depressingly dull. The air was heavy with a gray mist that settled on his skin in a greasy film. Calum shook the branches of a young tree. It swayed and bumped into a second tree, scratching the tree with its branches. The scratching became rhythmic as the second tree swayed and rocked into the next. Calum watched this pattern continue for a moment and then he turned to go back to the shed. He saw Laurel look around the corner of the small building. Her body became rigid and Calum sprinted back to her side.

"I see you've returned," said the voice of a boy who at that instant peered around the same corner at Laurel. His black hair gleamed like polished obsidian, and he had a dark complexion.

Laurel's hand instinctively found the pendant around her neck and she closed her fingers on it, too shocked to speak.

"Of course. You kept the token and figured out how to use it. Got here just in time, didn't you? The seven years are almost up." The boy smiled at her, showing a dimple on the right side of his face.

Calum was stunned, but managed one word.

"Finley?"

"Calum?" asked the boy. He shook his head in disbelief and looked again. "Is it really you?"

"Yes, it's me," said Calum. He hugged Finley tightly, nearly knocking him over. For a few minutes they were as two old friends greeting each other after a long separation. They hugged again and again and clapped each other's backs. Calum couldn't stop grinning.

"My parents. My sister…" said Finley, "are they all right?"

"They're fine," said Calum.

"And Hagen? He's not here, is he?" asked Finley, a note of panic in his voice.

"No, he's waiting for us to get back through," said Calum.

Finley looked relieved. "That's good, because that day, when they took me, it was a mistake. They were after Hagen."

"Why?" asked Laurel.

"Hagen is Torin's grandson," said Finley. "If he couldn't have Donnelly, he wanted to snatch Hagen so his rule could carry on."

"Hagen would never agree to do anything Torin asked," said Calum.

"Not now, but if they had gotten him when he was younger, things might have been different," said Finley.

Hagen. The thought of losing his cousin made Calum sick. This feeling was quickly replaced with anger. He *had* lost his cousin, he had lost Finley.

"We stayed in Ireland for a few months before Torin brought us to the Fairy Stone Mound in Virginia. That's where I met LaurelAnn." Finley smiled at her. "Daniel's told me all about you."

"My brother's here?" Laurel exclaimed.

"Yes," said Finley. "I'll take you to him."

Calum smiled at Laurel and took her hand. "It won't be long now." They followed Finley down the path to the village.

"If you were added," Calum almost choked on the word, "how come you're free, I mean, on your own?"

"Since the mound is sealed, there's no way I can escape," said Finley.

"Can't you use a token?" asked Laurel.

"If I had one," said Finley. He stopped walking and looked at her. "Every Sidhe gets just one token. If you lose it, you can't leave the mound unless you're taken out by another Sidhe."

"You've been trapped here because you gave me your token," said Laurel.

"Well, it wasn't mine for long," said Finley. "I only had it for a minute before I gave it to you."

"Thank you," said Laurel. She kissed Finley on the cheek. "Thank you for giving me a way to get back to my brother."

Finley blushed deeply and continued walking.

"Why did Torin go to the Fairy Stone clan?" asked Calum.

"When he was banished, he started looking for a new home," said Finley. "He'd heard about the Fairy Stone and thought they'd be an easy target. He took me there and told them I was his *son*," he said, looking repulsed. "At first, the Fairy Stone welcomed Torin and were cooperative with his suggestions for leadership. They even agreed to seal their threshold at his encouragement. But he made a huge mistake when he altered their token with the Hobayeth mark." He pointed to Laurel's pendant. "When the Fairy Stone Sidhe realized his true intentions, most of them fled the mound. One of the last to leave told me he could go out with his wife using her token. He said he wanted me to have his. I walked out of the circle just as Daniel walked into it."

"We were following a song," said Laurel.

"Yeah, that was Torin, calling everyone back to the mound," said Finley. "When Daniel was captured, I felt responsible. I wanted to help him, so I decided to go back for him. Then I saw you when you almost stepped into the circle. I gave you my token just in case you went looking for Daniel. The mound was in chaos. I thought for sure I could get another token and without anyone noticing grab Daniel and go back out. But there was no other token. Daniel and I were stuck. We stayed at Fairy Stone Mound until last summer. They finally got their act together and ran us out. Most of the Fairy Stone hated Torin, but some came with us when we moved here; there aren't many left in Fairy Stone now."

Calum noticed the foul-smelling air had become much worse, if that were even possible. He glanced at Laurel, who was scrunching her nose against the stench.

161

"Here, let me fix that," said Finley. He cupped his hands over Laurel's nose and murmured, "*Abeo*." He repeated the gesture with Calum.

Calum found he could breathe without smelling the horrid odor.

"We do that for the merchants when they come to trade," Finley explained.

Calum studied his cousin. He was so different from how Calum had remembered him. Of course he was—they all were. It had been seven years after all, but there was something else. Finley was only one year older than Calum, but somehow he seemed much, much older. All those years of living under Torin's rule had aged Finley.

They entered the middle of Devil's Peak Mound where, oddly, no one was about. "They're all hiding," said Finley. "They know you're here and don't know what to expect. You timed it right. Torin left for Ireland ten minutes ago. He left his idiot friend Brownshire in charge."

"We know him," said Calum. "I mean, we saw him." He explained how they had watched Uilleam search the woods that day.

"I'll bet Brownshire nearly wet himself when he ran into Uilleam." Finley laughed. "Torin's gotten everyone worked up, and frightened to death of Uilleam."

Calum looked confused.

"Are you ready for this? Torin and his wife tell everyone they are on the run from Uilleam. They make it sound like *they're* the victims. Brownshire's terrified of Uilleam," said Finley.

Calum shook his head slowly. "Unbelievable."

"Brownshire's turned out to be one of my biggest fans. He saw me get the token that day. When I came back into the mound, he told Torin I did so by choice. Brownshire's the one who convinced Torin I had truly become one of them," said Finley.

"Laurel, it should be easy for you to free Daniel. All you'll have to do is tell Brownshire you're Daniel's sister, and demand his freedom. The verse will be undone. Brownshire will have to release Daniel. He'll lose his powers if he doesn't."

"And what about you?" asked Laurel. "How will you be able to leave?"

"I haven't worked that out yet," said Finley. "Daniel will be free, but you can only take one person back with the token."

"I know how," said Calum. A grin swept over his face as he realized he would finally have peace about what happened that day so many years ago. "I can take you out." Calum explained his ring's protection. Finley's legs buckled and Calum caught him.

"I'm finally going home?" Tears glistened in his eyes.

"Yes cousin. You're coming home."

Devil's Peak Public House was an old building made of large gray stones and a black tar roof. They clambered up wide wooden steps into the entrance hall where the temperature felt like it had dropped ten degrees. Calum shivered as they passed by Sidhe stories carved into the walls. Unlike stories in the Tusatha Public House, these carvings were twisted in cruel letters that gouged the walls in an ungrateful manner. Calum stared at what seemed to be a scar in the wood.

"That's my name," explained Finley. "Every time Brownshire carves it, the wood seals itself over my name. *Blooderdon*," he said, shaking his head.

Calum thought this must be a Hobayeth phrase or saying. He didn't ask because he didn't want to know any of their ways. Once they were gone from this dark place, Calum never wanted to return.

Finley led them down the hallway. "Watch out for tricks while you're here and don't eat any red crackle.

"What?" asked Laurel.

"Red sugar pane. It's like the red part of a candy apple," said Finley. "A favorite treat of dark Sidhe. However, it's also a way to trap duine daonna. If you eat it, you'll be tricked into believing you never want to leave the mound."

"Take my hand, Laurel," said Calum. "And don't let go." They followed Finley as he pushed open double doors into a large and dimly lit room. A round and unattractive dwarf-like creature sat on a tall chair at the center of the room. His clothes were stained, brown, and old. The bronze skin of his belly drooped over his belt like mud sliding down a mountain. It was Brownshire, and on his left sat Daniel.

Chapter Fourteen

All or None

Calum felt Laurel pulling him as she quickened her pace to get to Daniel. "Don't," he said, holding fast to her hand. "We have to do this the right way."

"Brownshire," said Finley, "I found these two at the edge of the mound. This is Calum, from the Aessea clan."

"Welcome brother," said Brownshire. His voice was rough, like sandpaper on gravel.

Daniel stared at them. "LaurelAnn?" he asked in a choked voice.

"Hush it." Brownshire raised a thick hand to strike Daniel, who cringed. "And who is this duine daonna?"

"Go ahead," whispered Calum.

"I'm Laurel. I'm here for my brother, Daniel," she said firmly.

"You must be tired, Calum," said Brownshire, ignoring Laurel completely. "Basil, take this young brother to our best café for refreshment." He waved to a man on his right who wore a grass green suit. The man was so thin his beard had more width than he did. Basil touched his hand to his forehead in a salute to Calum.

"We need to deal with the duine daonna," said Brownshire.

"What do you mean, deal with?" asked Calum.

"Well, she claims Daniel is her brother," said Brownshire. "Before we release one of our own to her, we need to determine whether or not she's telling the truth."

"From what I can see," said Calum, "she's more a part of your clan than Daniel. She wears one of your tokens, and he has none."

Brownshire leaned forward in his seat and stared at the Fairy Stone around Laurel's neck. "That's one of our old tokens. How did you get it?" he asked.

"How does anyone get a token?" asked Calum. "She wears your token, so she must be accepted by you and treated like one of your clan."

"Do not presume you know more about Sidhe traditions than I, young brother," Brownshire said in a warning tone. "I would tread lightly here if I were you."

"Do not presume me to be your brother," said Calum.

"You'd better watch your mouth," said Brownshire. His left hand cut through the air, and Calum felt a sting on the right side of his face. His cheek throbbed with a rising welt.

"Now sit down and show some manners," commanded Brownshire.

There was a loud scraping noise. Two massive chairs with lion's heads carved into the end of each arm slid across the floor, stopping directly behind Calum and Laurel. Laurel sat down, but Calum made no move, staring defiantly into Brownshire's droopy face.

"I said sit!" Brownshire raised his hand and cut the air again. Calum felt a slash on his right thigh. He grabbed his leg, looking down where his jeans had been sliced open by an invisible knife. Calum held back a scream. Blood seeped from his leg, staining the edges of the tear in his jeans. Another wave of Brownshire's hand knocked Calum into the seat behind him, the chair nearly tipping over from the force. The small lion's heads on the chair came to life, roaring and flashing tiny sharp teeth. Calum glanced at Laurel, who looked pale and close to fainting.

"Very good, Brownshire," said Finley, trying to calm the situation. "Shall I escort them back to the edge of the mound? Their time here is limited."

"No," said Brownshire. "We have plenty of time. Let them wait as our guests while we conduct our hearing." He looked at Calum. "Oh, you're bleeding. How'd that happen?" He waved his left hand and a bandage appeared on Calum's leg. "I'm afraid you might feel a slight sting from the medicine." He leaned forward, eagerly watching Calum for a reaction.

Calum's leg burned like fire. He grimaced from the pain, but refused to make a sound.

"Oh, you're no fun," said Brownshire. He turned to Finley. "Take them to the guest house and wait with them until you are called."

Finley stood still as a statue.

Calum whispered to Laurel, "It's not really a guest house. It's a holding cell and Finley has to use his token to get in."

"Do as you're told," growled Brownshire. He looked at Finley with raised eyebrows. Somehow his tiny brain understood Finley didn't have his token. He tilted his head slightly like a dog listening to a whistle. "Where is your token?" He looked slowly

167

from Finley to Laurel. Calum could see Brownshire working it out. "She has your token. You gave it to her, and in doing so, you have betrayed your clan."

"I have never betrayed my clan. For as you know, this is not my clan." Finley glared at Brownshire.

Brownshire's face turned deep red, the veins in his neck standing out.

Calum felt a static charge fill the air.

"*Fero tuti latum!*" shouted Brownshire.

There was a loud thunderclap, and time stood still. Time enough for Calum to look into Finley's eyes and see his terror. Finley understood what was happening to him. Calum tried to get up, but the lion's jaws snapped close to his chest. Calum didn't feel their razor-sharp teeth as they cut through his shirt, grazing his skin. He was engulfed in horror as he watched Finley slowly vanish in yellow smoke. Calum felt sick. It was hard to breathe. *What happened? Am I in a nightmare? How will I ever explain this to Finley's mom? He's really gone this time.*

"Finley!" screamed Daniel.

Daniel's cry brought Calum back to his senses. "Where is Finley?" he shouted.

"Gone," said Brownshire. "Sometimes these Additions are really more trouble than they're worth." He kicked Daniel, who fell to the ground. Laurel flinched, and the lions' heads on her chair whipped around, growling. Brownshire turned to Basil and said coldly, "Take all three of them to the guest house."

The lions' heads froze in place, allowing Calum and Laurel to stand up. Calum glanced at Laurel. She was petrified with fear.

"We have to go," he whispered to her. "Brownshire's not Sidhe. He doesn't respect our laws or he wouldn't have cut me or struck Finley down like that. If we don't move, he'll hurt or kill you and Daniel."

Laurel, Daniel, and Calum followed Basil through a long passageway to a stone building behind the Public House. Tears stained Daniel's cheeks as they approached the door to the building that looked more like a prison.

Basil opened the door. "Please make yourselves comfortable," he said sarcastically.

As soon as the door closed, Laurel ran to Daniel. He hugged her tightly as they cried in each other's arms. Calum thought they needed privacy. He waited for them in the kitchen, sitting at a rotted table. Thoughts of Finley swirled around Calum's head as bitter tears flowed down his cheeks. His thoughts were interrupted when Laurel and Daniel joined him at the table. He quickly wiped his face.

Laurel took Calum's hand. "I'm so sorry about Finley." Another sob escaped Daniel's throat. Laurel took his hand as well. "I'm sorry, Daniel. I know Finley took good care of you. But you're coming home now."

"How?" asked Daniel. "You don't know them. They're cruel. And smart."

"We're smarter," said Calum.

They waited together at the table, none of them eager to speak. Laurel held each of their hands in hers as time dragged by. Supper time had come and gone when Calum felt hunger growing in his belly. He noticed a flat dish of red crackle on the counter and wondered if it had the same effect on Sidhe as it did on duine daonna. *I'm not a duine daonna. I should be fine,* he silently reasoned. He approached the counter. The crackle glittered like rubies in the sun. *That looks delicious.* He wanted to touch the crackle, to taste it. Calum reached out his hand and applied a light pressure with his finger. The red crackle split into bite-sized pieces. That seemed like a fun thing to do, much like breaking plastic bubble wrap. He wanted to do it again.

"*Calum!*" Laurel shrieked.

Calum awoke from a dreamy state. He shook his head, clearing his mind. "That red crackle made me want to taste it. I thought I could, too, because I'm Sidhe. That was really stupid."

"It's okay. We're all hungry," said Laurel.

Calum realized they needed a distraction. "Daniel, what happened that day in the woods?" he asked.

"I passed into the mound as soon as I stepped into their circle. I had no idea I had traveled to another world," said Daniel. "Brownshire grabbed me by the back of my shirt and brought me to Public House. Torin was there. He conducted my hearing. It was simple. I came to their mound uninvited. In their line of thinking that made me fair game to be added to the clan.

"I kept asking about you, Laurel, and Mom and Dad. I'll never forget what Torin said: 'If your parents cared about you at all, they never would have allowed you to wander into the woods without them.' I've hated Torin ever since." Daniel paused a few seconds, his hands shaking with anger.

"When Finley came back that day, they thought he was choosing to live here. I was taken to his house as an Addition, a reward for Finley's loyalty. He took care of me and taught me about the Sidhe. We used to stay up late at night planning our escape, but we promised not to leave the mound without the other. He never told me he gave you that token." Daniel nodded at Laurel's pendant.

They heard a *click* and the front door of the house opened. It was Basil. "Come with me."

They followed Basil out of the house and back through the Public House. Calum's stomach lurched when he saw the scar in the wood that had healed over Finley's name was now completely gone. Smoothed over as if Finley had never been there at all. They continued walking through the mound. Calum realized they were going to the shed where he and Laurel had first entered Devil's Peak. Brownshire waited beside the crystal Calum had tied to the gate post almost an hour earlier. The moon was large and low on the horizon. Its silver light cast distorted shadows on the wet ground.

"I've made a decision," said Brownshire.

Or, maybe you've learned how to tell time, thought Calum.

"When that dreadful ban on Additions was passed again, the visitor time limit was changed," said Brownshire. "Calum, you may stay here for only one hour because you are Sidhe. I wonder why they did that."

"You know why." Calum glared at Brownshire.

"Oh yes," Brownshire said in a dismissive manner. "Finley. Anyway, the visitor time limit does not extend to *her*," he nodded at Laurel, "because she's duine daonna. However, she may leave anytime she likes because she has our token. Alas, the token also

171

allows her to come back anytime she would like. Although, I would strongly advise against it," he said with a greasy grin. "There is no provision for Daniel, just an antiquated tradition, one our clan does not practice. And the good news is, in a few short weeks he won't ever want to leave."

Laurel turned a deep shade of red. Anger came from her body in almost visible waves. She looked murderous, much the way Calum knew his grandfather would look when he learned about Finley.

That's it.

Finley's voice echoed in Calum's head. *Brownshire's terrified of Uilleam.*

"In that case, I think we'll take Daniel now," said Calum.

"Were you not listening, young brother?" asked Brownshire. "We have decided to keep Daniel here with us."

"Were *you* not listening?" asked Calum. "I told you I am not your brother. If we leave today without Daniel, Laurel will come back tomorrow with my grandfather. I believe you met him at Fairy Stone Park. His name is Uilleam Lindsey. He'll be eager to see you again, especially after I tell him what you did to Finley." Calum paused to allow the idea to sink into Brownshire's head. "I think we should swap. You give us Daniel, and we'll give you her token. But you need to decide fast." Calum looked at his watch. "You have about a minute to make up your mind because in two minutes she's leaving with me." He took Laurel's hand. "It's always about choices. Make yours."

Now it was Brownshire who turned blood red. He glared at Calum. Brownshire and Basil spoke in quick low voices.

172

"What are you doing?" hissed Daniel. "Take LaurelAnn and get out of here."

"Don't worry," whispered Calum. "She left one of her gloves in their circle. She can get out without the token. I'll take you back with my ring." He turned to Laurel. "After you give him the token, run through the gate. We'll be right behind you."

"Okay," said Laurel. Daniel looked unconvinced. Laurel gave him a quick hug. "I'll be fine."

"I don't like this," said Daniel.

"It is agreed," said Brownshire, interrupting Daniel's protests. Laurel stared into Brownshire's eyes. Showing no fear, she took the pendant from her neck. She hesitated, whispering to Calum, "There's got to be another way. I want to come back here and help the Fairy Stone get rid of Brownshire and Torin."

"There is no other way. We're running out of time," said Calum. "Do it now."

At the last possible second, Laurel dropped the token into Brownshire's stubby hand. It slipped through his fingers, and thudded to the ground.

"Fool," said Brownshire. "Did you really think we didn't know about your glove? That has been taken care of." He burst into cruel laughter. "All in all, it's been a good day," he said. "True, we lost Finley, but maybe we'll get to keep Laurel." He bent to pick up the token. "It's really too bad you don't know how to block thoughts, Calum. I know about your ring. Pity, it only allows for one co-traveler. As you said, it is always about choices. I wonder who you'll choose to take home with you."

Calum felt his stomach drop and a sense of despair washed

173

over him. *What have I done?* He looked at Laurel. She mouthed the words, "Take Daniel."

Then Calum noticed two things. Brownshire couldn't lift the token from the ground. And they were no longer in Devil's Peak.

"Where are we?" asked Laurel. She held Daniel's hand tightly.

"We're in the polder," said Calum, looking around the woods. Dozens of bittersweet berries littered the ground. "But we should be in their circle."

Uilleam stood a few yards away.

"Uilleam!" shouted Calum, running to him. "Finley was there," he said, sobbing into his grandfather's chest. "I'm sorry, I couldn't bring him back, and now he's gone forever. We shouldn't have gone."

"Calm yourself, son." Uilleam looked at Calum's bloodied jeans and shirt, and a quiet anger swept over him. "Are you all right?" he asked calmly. "What's happened to your leg, your chest?"

"I'm okay," said Calum. "But where's Hagen?" he asked, looking around wildly.

Hagen appeared at that moment. "I waited until the hour was up. I was just about to call Donnelly when I was pulled here."

"That was my doing," said Uilleam. "And now that everyone is back, we're going home. I'm not the only one who wants to hear about your trip to Devil's Peak."

"It's about time," said Kenzie when they walked through the door. She sat between Gus and Salena in the Ranson kitchen. Her face was a mixture of fear and anger. "Calum, I sure hope you like your room because you won't be seeing much else for the next few months." She froze when her gaze found the blood on Calum's jeans. "Oh, no! Are you okay?"

"I'm fine," said Calum. He hugged Kenzie, relieved to be home.

Kenzie's face softened. "Are you sure you're all right?"

Calum nodded. "Mom, this is Laurel's brother, Daniel." Daniel smiled shyly.

"We're glad you're here," said Kenzie, smiling back at him.

"Where's Dad?" asked Hagen.

"He heard the Hobayeth call while we were in Aessea," Tullia said cautiously. "He's investigating their mound."

"No!" cried Hagen.

"Donnelly will be all right," Uilleam said impatiently. "But right now, we need Aine and Connor. Their grandson was at Devil's Peak Mound."

Tullia collapsed onto a chair. "What?" she exclaimed. "Finley was there?"

Calum tried to close his mind, but it was too late.

"Torin wanted *Hagen*?" Tullia shrieked.

"Tullia, calm down. Hagen is safe, please concentrate. Call your parents to you," said Uilleam in a firm tone. "We'll sort through this when they get here."

Tullia did as Uilleam asked and then turned to Hagen. "Go upstairs and tell Brytes and Will everyone is safe. But don't mention Finley. And don't tell them where your father has gone."

Hagen didn't move. *Torin wanted me?*

Calum didn't have time to answer.

"Go," Tullia demanded.

Hagen snapped out of his fog and left the room.

"What is it?" Aine asked when she abruptly crossed the Ranson threshold. "I have never been summoned here before. What's going on?"

She was closely followed by Connor, worry etched in his every movement. Aine knelt to study her daughter's face.

"Finley was at Devil's Peak Mound," said Uilleam. Aine shot to her feet.

Uilleam caught her by the arm. "He's not there now. Let's go into the family room. We need to hear Calum's story."

CHAPTER FIFTEEN

FINLEY

Calum followed the others into the family room where Kenzie had already conjured cups of steaming chamomile tea. He took one and sat on the couch beside Aine. Calum sipped the tea, trying to compose himself. He took a deep breath and said, "Finley was the first person we saw when we got there." Aine patted Calum's shoulder lightly. Hagen entered the room as Calum continued. "He brought us to their Public House where Brownshire was acting in Torin's place." Calum eyed Aine for a reaction, but saw none.

"Ah, the brownie I met at Fairy Stone Park," said Uilleam.

"Yes," said Calum. "Brownshire figured out Finley had given his token to Laurel. And then he killed Finley." Aine was now looking quite pale.

"We shouldn't have gone. I'm sorry," said Calum.

"How do you know he killed him?" asked Uilleam.

"He said, '*fero tuti latum.*' Then there was a loud sound like thunder, and Finley disappeared in yellow smoke."

"Repeat that please, Calum," said Connor. "Repeat exactly what Brownshire said."

"*Fero tuti latum.*"

"Calum," said Uilleam. "I do not think Finley is dead."

"I saw him," said Calum. "And Brownshire said he was gone."

"Think, child," said Uilleam. "Would Aine and Connor be here if Finley were dead? Would Tullia? Would Hagen?"

Calum looked puzzled.

"None of them would be here," said Uilleam. "Because none of them *could* be here."

If Finley were dead, all of his clan would be called back to Tusatha for the Grand Call.

"Finley's alive." Calum's voice trembled with relief. He noticed this didn't seem to comfort Aine. And Calum couldn't shake a renewed sense of urgency in finding Finley. Something was terribly wrong. "Then what happened to him?"

"I'm not sure," said Uilleam. "*Fero tuti latum* is a dark verse. It means to carry. But I don't know what it means when spoken by a brownie."

"Dara and Liam must be told about Finley," said Aine.

Calum felt nauseous. *Dara. What's going to happen to her when she hears about this? Will she ever be able to forgive me? This is the second time Finley has disappeared. And I'm to blame again.*

Calum's grandmother sat beside him. "No, you're not," Salena said, taking his hand.

Kenzie took his teacup, refilled it with warm tea, and handed it back to him.

"When we were at the polder, I saw bittersweet berries on the ground," said Calum, taking the cup. "Were you watching us?"

"Yes. I watched until you reached their circle. I lost you after you crossed into their mound," said Uilleam.

"Then how did you know to get us out of there?" asked Calum.

"What the mind knows and sees is eclipsed by what the heart loves and needs," said Uilleam, smiling at his grandson.

"We must get back to Tusatha," Aine said quietly.

"We'll go with you," said Uilleam. He and Salena kissed Calum and Kenzie goodbye and hugged Gus. They followed Aine and Connor back to the threshold in the kitchen.

"I hope it's okay if we stay here until Donnelly gets back," said Tullia.

"I'd have it no other way," said Kenzie.

"Don't take this wrong," Daniel said haltingly, "but I really want to go home." Tears rolled down his cheeks and Laurel took his hand.

"Of course you do," said Kenzie in a kind voice, moving to rest her hand on his shoulder. "But I don't think we should move about in the open until Donnelly returns. Can you hold out just a little longer?"

Daniel nodded.

"Good. For now, I think we could all use a little rest," said Kenzie. "Take them upstairs, son."

Calum led Hagen, Laurel, and Daniel through the family room. There was a tinkling sound when Daniel bumped into the shelf where the Particulars were kept. He nearly knocked the vase over as he tried to set it right.

"Don't worry about those," said Kenzie.

"Mrs. Ranson, would it be all right if Daniel and I stay in the same room?" asked Laurel.

"I think that'd be fine," said Kenzie. "Go ahead and take Daniel up. I'll put Brytes in with Tullia."

Calum, Hagen, and Kenzie continued to Calum's room where the boys plopped down on the beds. "I'm so proud of both of you," she said. She took the dressing off Calum's leg and looked through the torn blue jeans. "You're completely healed. He knew better than to really hurt you," she said with a glint in her eye.

"But I lost Finley. It's my fault again," said Calum amid fresh tears. "I should have brought him home."

"You didn't lose Finley," said Kenzie. "You weren't responsible all those years ago and you're not responsible tonight. Torin must have put something into your eye that day. You were in terrible pain when Hagen brought you into the house. Today was no more your fault. You had no control over what Brownshire did. Your dad and I were pretty upset when we figured out where you went today, but now we're just so thankful you're home safe. And if you hadn't gone, we may never have known what happened to Finley." She gently caressed his cheek. "Rest, child." She repeated this gesture with Hagen and both boys immediately fell into a deep sleep.

Calum and Hagen were the last to rise when they made their way downstairs the next morning.

"Good afternoon," Gus teased. He sat at the table with Kenzie and Tullia.

"Yes, good afternoon, son," said Donnelly. He leaned against the kitchen counter with a mug of coffee in his hand.

Hagen rushed to Donnelly and wrapped his arms around his father. "I was so worried about you."

"No need," said Donnelly. "I know all of their tricks."

Calum watched his uncle hold Hagen tightly to his chest. *Donnelly is a good man. How could I have doubted him?*

"What happened?" asked Hagen.

"I wish I knew," said Donnelly, joining the adults at the kitchen table. "I heard the call when we were at Iris' house. I went to the Hobayeth Mound to check it out." Hagen gave his father a worried look. "Don't worry, I wasn't recognized."

"Being a shape shifter has its benefits," Gus winked.

"Torin had been there, trying to get support to reverse the Additions Law when it comes up again," Donnelly said disgustedly.

"Did you see any of your family?" asked Kenzie.

"My mother and sisters were not at the mound."

"Well, at least we know where Torin is, or where he was," said Tullia.

"Yes, and he'll wish we didn't when I find him," said Donnelly. "It's a shame I didn't know about Finley before I went to the Hobayeth Mound."

"There'll be another time," said Gus.

"I'm glad you feel that way," said Donnelly. Gus looked puzzled at this remark.

"Emerald Lake is changing. You've been a part of our world long enough to know our magic. Our ways. It's high time you accepted our Gifts."

"I don't know," said Gus. "I like things this way. You know, you being able to kick my butt with magic, but me being able to kick yours without it."

Calum snickered at the thought of his father and uncle fighting like two kids.

"Well, that last part remains to be seen," said Donnelly. "But if you like, we can find out later. I'd hate to embarrass you in front of your son."

Gus laughed. "Dream on, Donnelly," he said.

"Seriously, we need you. I don't think you appreciate who I am, who my father is," said Donnelly. "They're going to look for me. We can call Uilleam here tonight and he can perform the Ceremony of the Three Clans with me and Tullia."

The Ceremony of the Three Clans. Calum realized his father would receive Gifts from the Aessea, Tusatha, and Hobayeth clans. *The Hobayeth. What's going to happen to Gus when he gets their blood? Why can't Kenzie do it instead of Donnelly?*

"Spouses can't give the Gifts," said Donnelly quietly, without judgment.

Calum felt ashamed. He looked at all of the adult Sidhe in the room and hoped no one else had heard his thoughts. Everyone was caught up in the possibility of Gus receiving the Gifts and hadn't seemed to notice Calum's interaction with his uncle.

"I'll think about it," said Gus.

"Don't wait too long," said Donnelly.

Gus looked at his watch. "We're supposed to have Laurel back in an hour," he said. "How are we going to explain Daniel?"

"We can adjust their memories," said Donnelly. "I can make

it so they'll believe they never met any of us."

"No," Calum begged. "Donnelly, please don't." He couldn't bear another loss, not so soon after losing Finley again.

Kenzie patted Calum's shoulder. "I think you spent too much time with the Hobayeth yesterday, Donnelly," she said. "But even if you adjusted their memories, what could we do about Daniel? He lived in that clan for almost seven years. What memory would replace that time? There really is no other explanation but the truth."

"Okay," said Donnelly. "We tell them the truth about Daniel's disappearance and where he's been. However, we leave out the rest, our Sidhe background, and the fact that Calum and Laurel retrieved him."

"Of course," said Kenzie. "We live among them, but we are not of them. So how do we get Daniel home and still keep our secret?"

"Not how. Who." Donnelly grinned. "I think it's about time Mr. Girvan earned his salary."

"Like I said, being a shape shifter has its benefits," said Gus.

𝒲𝒾

Calum carried Laurel's bag to the truck and put it on the back seat. "Are you up to this, Laurel?"

"I've never been good at acting," she said. "But they're going to be so happy about having Daniel home, they won't notice."

"Donnelly just got back," said Kenzie, climbing into the truck. "It's all set. Let's go."

183

They drove the short distance to Laurel's house. "Thanks again, for everything," said Laurel. "We would never have gotten Daniel back without your help."

"It's the least we could do," said Kenzie.

"And don't worry," said Laurel. "I won't tell anyone about you guys."

"We know you won't," said Gus.

Calum stared out of the window in silence.

"Finley's next, Calum." Laurel squeezed his hand. "I know he is."

They arrived at Laurel's house, unloaded the truck, and approached the door.

"Laurel!" called Andrea, running down the steps to greet them. "It's Daniel. Mr. Girvan just brought him home."

Laurel rushed into her mother's arms. They climbed the steps together and entered the house. Calum and his parents left Laurel's things inside the door and slipped away unnoticed.

W

The next evening, the Dunbars and Werners gathered for a "welcome home" cookout at the Ranson house. Daniel told everyone the details of his kidnapping and described the years he spent with the Hobayeth. Calum tried to look like this was news to him.

"I know it sounds crazy," said Andrea. "But Daniel swears he was taken by fairies and has been living with them all these years."

She nervously studied Kenzie's face for a reaction.

"Come on," said Kenzie. "You're from Virginia. You mean to tell me you've never heard about the Fairy Stone clan?"

"Well, sure." Rob shrugged. "But I thought that was just a local superstition. A story someone made up to boost tourism."

"Then how do you explain the fairy stones?" asked Gus. "They're all over the park."

"I don't know," said Rob.

"I keep telling myself it can't be true, but when Daniel talks about it, I believe him," said Andrea.

"The important thing is, Daniel's home," said Donnelly. He looked first into Andrea's eyes and then into Rob's.

The Werners' eyes glazed over. "Yes," said Rob, "the important thing is Daniel's home."

"That's right," said Andrea, staring trance-like at Donnelly. "The important thing is Daniel's home."

Donnelly looked away, and the Werners snapped out of their stupor. They looked dazed, but perked up when Donnelly said, "There's a bottle of champagne waiting for us in the fridge. Let's celebrate."

The adults went inside, and Calum, Hagen, and Laurel filled Daniel in on life in Emerald Lake. "Basically, it's a small town, where everyone knows everyone else," said Calum.

"And they mean *everyone*," Laurel added.

"Except that girl I saw at Devil's Peak circle," said Hagen.

"You weren't supposed to follow us to their circle," said Calum.

185

"You aren't really surprised that I did. Are you?" Hagen asked with a sly grin. Calum shook his head. "Anyway, she saw me and ran for it. I chased that girl all over the reserve. We ended up back at the circle. And then she disappeared."

"Is that when she took Laurel's glove?" asked Calum.

"She never got it." Hagen dropped Laurel's glove on the table. He glanced at Daniel. "Is there something you want?"

"I'm sorry, I don't mean to stare. It's just that you look so much like Finley," said Daniel.

"So I've heard," said Hagen, smiling at Laurel. "I wish I could have seen him. I really do."

"I'm sorry you didn't get the chance," said Daniel.

"You have nothing to be sorry about," said Hagen. "It was Brownshire's doing, and believe me, he'll pay for it." In that second, Calum thought Hagen looked just like his father.

"Still, I wonder," said Laurel. "How did we get to the polder?"

"We got there when Uilleam called us to him," said Calum.

"Okay, but since when can Uilleam call a duine daonna?"

"I don't know. There are a lot of things I don't understand about my grandfather," said Calum. "But I do know his magic is very strong."

"I'm just glad I'm home with LaurelAnn," said Daniel. "I mean, Laurel."

"It's okay," said Laurel. "I like it when you call me LaurelAnn."

"Daniel, you must have heard tons of verses in that clan," said Hagen. "Maybe you can teach us some before school starts."

"I learned all kinds of verse, good and bad," said Daniel. "Finley..." He fell silent for a moment, then continued in a stronger voice. "Finley taught me. I memorized all of their verses, but I could never get the hang of it. Strange, toward the end it seemed the verses were working. Then again, maybe Finley was doing the magic and I only thought it was me."

CHAPTER SIXTEEN

SCHOOL'S OUT

The last day of school finally arrived. Lockers were cleaned out, books had been returned, and farewells said to friends and teachers. Calum, Hagan, Laurel, and Daniel sat together in the main gym for the sixth-grade awards ceremony. Their parents watched from the bleachers, with the exception of Rob, who was on the stage with the sixth-grade teachers. Red-and-white balloons decorated the stage, and bushy green plants sat at both ends of long tables. Medals, pins, and stacks of certificates waited for distribution.

Calum leaned over to Laurel. "Riley isn't here."

"Yeah, I heard her talking to Brenna. She said her mom was going to take her to the beach because we weren't going to do anything important in school today. The truth is Riley got a D in PE so she isn't on the Honor Roll."

"How in the world do you get a D in PE?" asked Hagen.

"Well, Riley never dressed out," Laurel replied. "She said the PE uniform was tacky and there was no way she would wear one."

"Good grief," said Daniel. "She sure is high maintenance."

The local Boy Scout troop served as the Color Guard. All

conversation came to an end as they carried the US and North Carolina flags into the gym. Everyone stood and recited the Pledge of Allegiance. Next, Rob approached the podium and thanked all the parents for coming and for their support during his first year at Longwood Middle School.

Students were called to the stage one at a time and recognized for their achievements. Calum and Hagen received perfect attendance certificates. Calum and Laurel received medals for being on the A Honor Roll for the entire year, and Hagen received a pin for being on the A/B Honor Roll. Calum won the highest academic average in math, and Laurel was surprised when she received the highest academic average in science.

After the ceremony, Andrea took several pictures of the four friends with their teachers. Calum's mom hugged him, and his dad shook his hand before pulling him into a bear hug. Both parents were beaming with pride, and Calum obliged them one picture.

It took a long time for the gym to empty, and when it finally did, students ran outside for their end of the year picnic. A local caterer was on campus, and the air was fragrant with the smell of hamburgers sizzling on their large portable grill. Calum, Hagen, Laurel, and Daniel filled their plates and found seats at the same table as Barry, Kirby, and Susie. After they finished their meal, they played water balloon relay, freeze tag, and bucket brigade, a game in which students used buckets of water to put out small controlled fires. Students were hot and tired when they were told to return to the sixth-grade hall one last time.

Ms. Itig hugged them, and told them goodbye as they entered her classroom. "There won't be time for goodbyes later," she said.

"That was weird," said Hagen.

"Not for her," Calum said with an appreciation for his favorite teacher's quirky behaviors.

For their final assignment, Ms. Itig commissioned her students to create bookmarks for her next batch of sixth graders. These were two-sided creations. One side welcomed the new student, and the other side offered tips on surviving their first year in middle school.

As they worked, Susie Turnbill's hand shot up in the air.

"Yes, Susie." said Ms. Itig.

"I heard you used to teach seventh grade."

"That's true."

"Well, I was wondering if you would move up to seventh grade and teach us next year," said Susie.

"Absolutely not," said Ms. Itig.

Ignoring all rules about blurting out, students asked, "Why?" and pleaded, "Come on, Ms. Itig."

"I don't like seventh graders," she replied.

Several students cried out, "Why not?"

"Because they are horrible, horrible children," said Ms. Itig.

"But don't you think you'll like us?" asked Kirby.

"I barely like you now. What makes you think I'll like you then, for heaven's sake?"

It was hard to tell if Ms. Itig was joking or not. And that was her way. Calum had learned many things from Ms. Itig and one of them was humor. Calum realized it had taken him an entire year to figure out that Ms. Itig really did like her students. They just needed a year to grow to like her.

The students continued working on their bookmarks, and when they finished, put them into Ms. Itig's basket. They cleaned up their areas, and sat talking and signing yearbooks as they waited for the end of the day. Some students stopped by Ms. Itig's desk and gave her fierce hugs. The final few minutes of the school year were evaporating like dew on an early spring morning when a long and mournful sound came drifting down the hallway.

"What's that?" asked several students at once.

"That marks the end of your sixth-grade year," said Ms. Itig. "I wish you all a safe summer, and I hope you'll come visit me next year."

Then Ms. Itig did something strange, even for her. She picked up an old frying pan Calum recognized from their lessons about sound waves. Next she picked up a wooden spoon and used it to bang on the bottom of the pan. She ushered her students toward the door and into the hallway which was filled with resounding noise. The mournful sound turned out to be bagpipes being played by the band director as he led students from his classroom.

All of the teachers were making noise with various objects. Some were playing actual instruments and others, like Ms. Itig, who were clearly nonmusical, were making noise with pots and pans. The teachers marched students through the school, out the front door, and to the buses. They continued to serenade their students, and waved goodbye to each bus as it drove out of the parking lot.

Kenzie waited for Calum and his friends in the car line. The four friends climbed into the car, and Calum turned around to take one last look at Longwood Middle School as they drove out of the parking lot. He wasn't sure, but the teachers seemed to be dancing in a long, winding conga line as they made their way back into the building.

"How many friends are coming to Siopa Leabhar for the patio party?" asked Kenzie.

"About twelve, counting us," said Calum.

"Well everything's ready for you. Let me know when you want me to bring out the refreshments."

"Thanks, Mom."

Calum, Hagen, Laurel, and Daniel entered Siopa Leabhar and were greeted by Wrecks. He had been waiting for them on the window seat and howled loudly when he glimpsed their arrival.

"Hey, boy," said Calum. "Are you ready for summer vacation? I am."

"Laurel, may I see you for a second?" asked Kenzie.

The boys walked outside to the patio, with Wrecks following closely with his ever-wagging tail. They sat at one of the tables and reflected on their sixth-grade year as they waited for their classmates to arrive.

"Remember how afraid we were to go to Longwood? It seems stupid now," said Calum.

"Speak for yourself," said Hagen. "I wasn't afraid."

Calum burst out laughing. "Yes you were."

"Yeah, yeah," said Hagen. Then he changed the subject by asking, "Did you get a look at the seventh grade summer reading list? It has *three* books. Honestly, do they expect us to walk around with our nose in a book all summer?"

"And I have one more," said Laurel, joining them. "Kenzie just gave me this." She handed a worn leather-bound book to Calum.

He read the title and smiled. "*A Broken Accord.* Mom's favorite book." At that moment, Calum knew Laurel had been accepted into their clan. Daniel, too. No question. Finley had treated Daniel as his brother, and so would Calum.

"Hey, do you guys know where I can buy the summer reading books?" asked Hagen with a laugh.

Wi

Calum spent the first week of summer vacation as he had done so many years before, working at Siopa Leabhar. This summer, however, he had a new purpose. He sat at the checkout desk reading an ancient book, surrounded by at least twenty other volumes of varying sizes. All looked to be centuries old with crusty covers and threadbare bindings.

"Read much?" asked Hagen, wandering into the store. "Where'd you get those old books?"

"Some came from Uilleam, and some from our leabharlann," said Calum. "I thought I might find something about brownies."

"And their verse," Hagen said with complete understanding. "Hand me one."

"Thanks for helping," said Calum, passing one of the thick books to Hagen.

"He's my cousin, too."

"This is the third time I've tried to read this part. As soon as I read it, I forget what I've read. It's like the book doesn't want me to know."

"Maybe that's how it keeps its secrets," said Hagen.

The two boys read in silence until it was time to close the store. Calum returned the dusty books to a glass display case labeled Collectibles. He stepped through the stacks, picking up and putting away stray books and magazines. *Maybe tomorrow*, he thought. *I'll never stop looking, Finley. I promise.*

A soft orange light glowed from one of the stacks and then dimmed as Calum followed his mother and cousin outside.

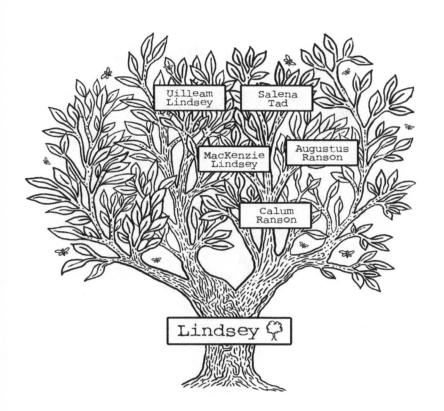

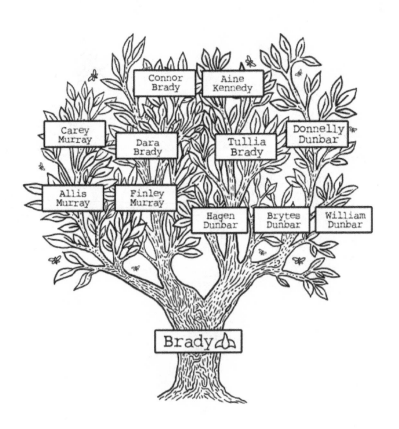

THE CHOICE
BOOK TWO OF THE SIDHE

CHAPTER ONE
ALMOST MISSED IT

"Are you sure you saw it?" Calum asked, running his hand through his light brown hair. "You saw the glowing?"

"Yes," Hagen puffed. "I'm positive, cuz."

"Kenzie, what's taking so long?" Calum impatiently bounced on the balls of his feet in front of Siopa Leabhar.

"I'm hurrying," said Kenzie. She struggled with the lock on the heavy door to the only bookstore in Wander County. "It's stuck."

"Forget the lock!" said Calum. "*Pateface!*" He tore into the bookstore, Hagen close behind him. "Come *on*, Hagen. Show me!"

Granddad, Calum thought as he raced to the back of the store. *I need you.* He was met at the cash register by a tall man with copper-colored hair.

"What is it?" asked Uilleam. "Why did you call me here? What's wrong?"

"Hagen saw the glowing," Calum said breathlessly.

"I saw it just before Kenzie closed the door when we were leaving," explained Hagen.

"Are you sure it was meant for you?" asked Uilleam.

"We were the only ones here," said Calum. "It has to be the verse for Finley." He raced erratically from stack to stack, pulling books from the shelves, exposing hundreds of lines of faerie verse. "Help me move the books so we can see them," he urged.

"Stop, Calum," Uilleam said calmly. He raised his right arm and swept the air, causing the books to return their places.

Calum looked at his grandfather in disbelief. "But we have to find it," he pleaded.

"We *will* find it," said Uilleam. "What was the last thing you were doing before you closed the bookshop?"

Calum breathed deeply, trying to remember. "Hagen and I were going through those old books you gave me, looking for the translation of Brownshire's verse. It was time to go home. Mom and Hagen waited at the front door while I put the books in here."

Calum walked to a glass display case labeled Collectibles. "*Pateface*," he said, peering inside. "Wait a minute. That wasn't there before." The letters *Wi* had been carved into the wood hundreds of times, spilling down the front of the shelf, stopping just above a thin green book with no title. "It has to be this one." Calum pulled the book from the shelf. "But it can't be."

"Why not?" asked Uilleam.

"I already tried to read this book, but the words don't make sense." He passed the book to his grandfather.

"I haven't seen one of these in years," said Uilleam, turning the volume over in his hands.

"You know this?" asked Kenzie.

"Yes," said Uilleam, flipping through the pages. "Switch Verse. It's very old, dark magic. Words are poured onto the page from a lepidolite cup, which protects the verse from being read."

"But *you* can read it, can't you, Granddad?" Calum asked desperately.

Uilleam smiled. He put the book on the checkout desk and opened to a random page in the middle. Passing his hand over the book, he said, "*Oriri.*" The book shook and clouds of dust wafted up from it.

Calum watched as words made their way to the top of the page, rearranging themselves into coherent sentences. He felt Hagen edging closer to him, peering over his shoulder.

"It looks like a dictionary," said Hagen.

"A book of faerie verse," said Uilleam. "Probably in alphabetical order."

Calum turned the pages. Each was a jumbled mess of words, but within seconds, verses straightened themselves out on the yellowed pages. Calum turned several pages back. "Here it is!" he said. "That's what Brownshire said: *Fero tuti latum.*" Calum read the words aloud. "A dark and destructive verse. Not intended for killing; however, the accursed will wish for death, for the existence of a…" Calum squinted. "I can't make out the next word."

Kenzie leaned in, reading the passage. "Oh no," she gasped.

"Finley's been turned into a—"

"A what?" Calum sputtered. "What's happened to him?"

The look in Kenzie's eyes told him he didn't want to know, that he couldn't handle knowing. But another fear gripped Calum. If he couldn't even handle knowing the truth, how would Finley survive it?

ACKNOWLEDGEMENTS

I am blessed to have so many wonderful people in my life. I thank them now for their love and encouragement.

First, my Creator, without whom I would have nothing and be nothing.

I'd like to thank my husband, Andrew.

I thank my greatest joy, Connor, who amazes me and inspires me on a daily basis. Thank you to Stephanie for your support and encouragement in this writing thing and my heart to Clara for blessing us all with her beautiful light.

Heartfelt thanks to my parents Chuck and Jeri Cipriano. I simply could not have had better. And thank you to my number one cheerleader, Ruth Bullard.

Thanks to my brother, Charles Cipriano and sister, AnnMarie Cipriano Phillips and my bonus siblings, Kristi and Greg. Thank you for my beautiful nieces and nephews, each of whom holds a special place in my heart. Kristin (and Jared), Mary (and Nick), Trey (and Sunny), Preston, Sarah, Karen, Hannah, Harry, Emily, and Megan.

I love you all.

To ZiZi, my constant companion and bedtime alarm clock, I love you because, well you know why. Sweet dreams, Kitten.

Special thanks to Sarah Hembrow, my wonderful and patient editor. We've really got our hands full now with two series and I couldn't keep them straight without you! Big thanks to Rob Johnson and Vulpine Press for giving *The Sidhe* a wonderful home. Thank you to Claire Wood for the beautiful cover artwork.

And a huge thank you to my readers. I love hearing from you, so please do reach out and let me know what you think about Calum, Hagen, Laurel and everyone at Emerald Lake ☺

Website	www.cindycipriano.com
Instagram	therealcindycipriano
Facebook	@VictorLeathJames
Twitter	@CindyCipriano

CPSIA information can be obtained
at www.ICGtesting.com
Printed in the USA
BVHW030716120620
581245BV00004B/171

9 781912 701681